D1476459

STRANGE
TRAFFIC

ALSO BY IRENE DISCHE

Pious Secrets

The sun, whose neutral eye
all florid August from the sky,
had watched the earth behave
and seen strange traffic on her brown and green.

—W. H. Auden

STRANGE TRAFFIC

Stories

Irene Dische

Metropolitan Books

Henry Holt and Company / New York

Metropolitan Books
Henry Holt and Company, Inc.
Publishers since 1866
115 West 18th Street
New York, New York 10011

Metropolitan Books℠ is a division of Rowohlt
and an imprint of Henry Holt and Company, Inc.

Published in Canada by Fitzhenry & Whiteside Ltd.,
195 Allstate Parkway, Markham, Ontario L3R 4T8.

Library of Congress Cataloging-in-Publication Data
Dische, Irene.
Strange traffic: stories/Irene Dische.—1st ed.
p. cm.
1. Manners and customs—Fiction. I. Title.
PS3554.I825S77   1995   95-7635
813'.54—dc20   CIP

ISBN 0-8050-4172-9

Henry Holt books are available for special promotions
and premiums. For details contact: Director, Special Markets.

First Edition—1995

Design by Betty Lew

Printed in the United States of America
All first editions are printed on acid-free paper.∞

1 2 3 4 5 6 7 8 9 10

Contents

A Prior

Engagement

1. Gossip, Philosophy, and Other Forms of Beating Around the Bush

When Oliver Weinstock reached that point in the conversation when his partner's resistance to mental intrusion had crumbled, he lit a match and, holding it carefully as if it were a solitary candle lighting up the darkness, he said, "While the doctors shine their weak torches into the drain hole that is your past, I guess the direction your life has taken is the product of coincidence alone. This applies particularly to love. But mind you, what counts is not whom you loved or who loved you, but who did not love you. And," he concluded, "how they did not love you." He dropped the match, still burning, to the floor. It was coincidence that he had never started a fire that way.

. . . cold night, overheating in the city, . . . is Oliver? she shares a room with her grown-up son while her husband sleeps next door! has Oliver? he translated her angry letters from Russian, she had the pills, ready to, perhaps you are a poor kisser, he said to his student, Oliver says, *ein Spiel bei dem man nie gewinnt. . . .*

You might imagine that Oliver Weinstock was a dour, pessimistic sort of man, but far from it. He was one of those jolly regulars who patronize the snootier cafés in Berlin where you must know the owner to get a seat, or know one of her favorite, famous customers, or as a last resort, be the owner. In fact, he was an American, a New Yorker, but he had left New York because love was his hobby, he said, and love no longer really counted there —social status counted more. People married to get love over and done with, and after that it no longer crossed their minds.

His amusing pessimism, couched in that soft, silly American accent, was familiar to anyone who spent a few hours in his company. It was true, in Berlin love interested the café-going population inordinately, potential passion was felt smoldering in all relationships, while the dying of passion was expected, sniffed for, as soon as love publicly announced itself. In short, no conversation gave satisfaction unless it contained at least a passing mention of love's furies. Oliver Weinstock's contribution was always original, always worth listening to—the sudden ring of truth that began in the hum of gossip, rose, distinguished itself for a few phrases, and then disappeared.

. . . bildet sich was auf ihre Schönheit, the host is a bully, bullying the hostess, not a very pretty, sado-maso, the friends decide, but

maybe, Oliver thinks host's despotism keeps hostess young at heart, childlike, winsome, *dreht jeder, schwanz. . . .*

Weinstock's interpretation of love rested on the principle that rejection was much more important than affection. One was likely to be rejected soon enough into adulthood, and one's subsequent choice of love was a response to this rejection, an attempt to redress it. Perhaps one kicked the next person, only to be kicked in turn by another, kick, kicked; or one repeated one's behavior, hoping for a payoff. In any case, the heart remained tied down, while mind and body set out on a long search for exactly the same thing, until finally, sooner or later, one lost one's vitality and preferred security—oh, security was an emotion too!—sinking into boredom and apathy with whichever person, for whatever sorry reasons of their own, happened to have stuck to one's side.

Oliver Weinstock, who had no wife at his side . . . doesn't give the impression of looking for one, somehow . . . argued that his view made a lot of psychological heavy thinking unnecessary. In fact, in order to understand a man's nature, you must simply find out how his first serious love affair ended. He dodged the question of his own by shrugging his shoulders and saying, "First you tell me yours." His audience gladly obliged.

It was one of love's mysteries, Weinstock knew, that most people prefer hearing their own love stories, even though they know them rather well, to listening to others tell theirs. So Weinstock's conversations about love were a kind of 1,001 nights in which he never did the talking but elicited it from others. When pressed, he would hint at the affairs he was having or had had. He never confessed more than a tiny detail, but this was always a nonsequitur designed to shock and thereby hold up the listener's imagination, such as, "I had always wanted to have a woman's pump up my ass."

. . . sometimes I ask myself, I wonder whether he isn't a-, asex-, whether he isn't, just because he isn't married? he's rather, I wonder, noncommittal for all of his passionate interest in, no ties to his family in New York. . . .

Pressed further about his own experiences, he would tell an anecdote about his childhood. "I had six sisters," he often said, "the nearness of the word six to sex cannot be overlooked under these circumstances. My sisters used to take turns visiting me when I took a bath. The penis envy of six sisters—like being a Negro in a white family." Then he would add, with a modesty most unusual for his social surroundings, "My father's organ, of course, was massive, and I knew my place and admired it. That is where I developed my love for the monumental."

. . . one of his nice jokes! love isn't animated aesthetics with us: it is chemistry: it is chance! love is not, never, a demonstration of the natural tendency for things to dwindle, he's nice, Oliver's nice, few people are nice in this city. . . .

In short, Oliver Weinstock was one of the nicest people who ever lived. This category left him plenty of occasion for minor misdemeanors, such as his habit of playing with matches at the high point of a conversation. He was of medium size, with huge blue eyes. Even as a child his eyes had slight purple rings under them, which added to their expression of restrained intensity. His shoe-brown hair had, he complained, been "subjected to Delilah's invisible shears" at an early age, disappearing from his head soon after his very first love affair, an episode that had marked him, more than his relationship with his parents or with his many siblings. It had marked him forever—he would say no more. At that age, he had looked like a sad cherub; now he resembled a happy cleric. He was composed of soft lines beginning with that rounded, glistening pate, his face had no hard edges or ungainly bulges, his shoulders were curved, his hands were white and delicate.

. . . he's not handsome, not in any ordinary, but attractive, yes, very, . . .

Although he was horrendously knowledgeable about literature, theater, and art, he did not collect knowledge, hoard it, count it, lord it over others, as so many knowledgeable people do. He had a desire to make people happy, it was really his only ambition. To this end, he came when they called, he never turned down a request for help, and he was generous not only with his time but also with his admiration. He did not gossip, for fear of injuring others, he preferred to poke gentle fun at himself. When heads leaned together and the talk turned to love affairs, he confided that he was bad.

■ ■ ■

. . . of course he's not bad. . . .

He frowned and smiled simultaneously and said no more; it was someone else's turn to confess. He was full of good humor, he adored a joke and had a booming laugh, and he was, to quite a number of people, a best friend.

. . . don't forget to invite Oliver Weinstock. . . . saw him with, saw him with, yesterday, is there something? *vergnügt, unbesorgt,* did he say, something about liking shoes in his ass, *von Freud ist nicht die Rede,* don't believe. . . .

After arriving in Berlin as a young man, Oliver Weinstock did not seek the comforts of commitment. Instead he dabbled in close friendships and intellectual chores—he wrote small articles for small magazines, helped out at local museums—this brought him enough money to pay the rent and travel modestly. Sometime in his thirties, he reckoned that statistically his life was half over, and a sense of doom overcame him. At one party he was heard repeating, "The present provides protection against the terrors of the future, but not against the horrors of the past." He always kept a piece of paper in his breast pocket, along with a box of matches. He sometimes removed the box in order to light a match, but he never removed the paper. He had a habit of pulling it out slightly from the pocket and then pushing it back down again. Something he had written? A story, perhaps? And why shouldn't he? Nearly everyone does. Someone once claimed to have seen him actually remove this dog-eared page and read it. He had been sitting alone in a café. A few seconds passed, and then he folded it and tucked it back into his shirt pocket, minding it like a wallet.

. . . I asked him what it was, he said, My True Confessions, *allein ein Pergament,* it's damn short, I laughed, I think he's depressed, he's just not himself, but he does verbalize it. . . .

"Early disappointment causes deformation," he explained, "influencing the growth process, while disappointment late in life causes pain, all the more pain because the victim cannot accommodate it." He went on and on in this vein, "It is not the future that is limited when you know you are going to die, but the past." His concerned father intervened. On a brief visit from New York to introduce his new young wife, he bought Oliver a café of his own, centrally located, with a small apartment in the back.

Oliver Weinstock accepted gratefully. He turned a dark, dingy place into a clean, whitewalled restaurant with a selective, expensive menu and fine wine. He did not give it a name. He could not think of one. The matchboxes he had made for his business simply read, "Eat, Drink, and Be Merry." The diners always referred to "the Weinstock." His friends were delighted with the new arrangement. Now they knew where to find him every evening, they could count on a free bottle of wine or hors d'oeuvre, and their pleasure in his company increased. Weinstock proved a good businessman, without coming down with any of the usual side effects of success. He did not become a tightwad with his time and he remained a generous host; he hired a large staff but helped with the cooking and the menu and the shopping—he even waited tables himself. He made no distinction between friends, staff, and customers; in fact, he was utterly lacking in class consciousness.

. . . he's just more modern than we are, but it makes him helpless with his employees. Imagine if he didn't have Frau Bussjäger. . . .

Coincidence tossed him the Bussjägers, an elderly couple who always showed up very late at night, Frau Bussjäger boarded up for old age in costly clothes with an asphalt-colored wig on her head, while her husband was unkempt and unshaven, with spots on his suit. He liked Coca-Cola and habitually drank two glasses to start his meal. Then he would order several expensive items, but leave half his food untouched, because he preferred to smoke while looking down at his plate; his wife only wanted tea and a potato and, for dessert, an aspirin. They barely spoke. Their silence was so customary that it was Oliver Weinstock who noticed one evening what Frau Bussjäger had missed—her husband was not just being introverted, he had actually died. He ordered the restaurant crew to carry on as normal. "There's no telling how she will respond," he warned. "Her form of not speaking to her husband is a kind of chronic hysterical attack because of deep disappointment in him." He waited until all the other guests had left before calling an ambulance and letting the doctor give her the bad news. She took it very well, asking for another aspirin.

After this unhappy event she became a nightly guest, shyly consulting the menu before ordering her potato. She grew talkative and proved to be chock-full of interesting opinions about art, politics, and morals. "One mustn't read other people's mail," she often said. When asked about her husband, she always answered, "Married twenty-eight years, two months, and three days, all of it wonderful, every minute a miracle. We shared one mind and one nervous system."

. . . ha! ha! that puts us all to shame, doesn't it. . . .

One evening she went into the kitchen and told the chef that God's potatoes were fine-grained and smooth, while man-made potatoes were mealy, gummed up one's dentures. Eventually, Oliver Weinstock asked her whether she would help out in the restaurant. He did not like telling others what to do, and she seemed the ideal person to pass on his wishes to the staff.

. . . bet she'll have herself lifted now, *bedauerst sie!* don't find her appealing, true love does exist, it's been seen. . . .

Frau Bussjäger proved an excellent manager, a punctilious commander who gave orders with her eyes. And when his guests complained about her humorlessness, the way her head seemed to teem with moral and aesthetic judgments, her lips pressed shut to hold them back, Oliver Weinstock defended her, saying, "She is my friend" and then he promised them, "Someday I will ask her how her first love affair ended. Then we will know more."

Although she was much too reserved to show her feelings openly, she was obviously fond of her benefactor. She offered her affections from a great distance, and from a great distance he accepted them, which she figured was his way of returning them. Oliver behaved like a gentleman and a good son. He always walked her home after closing in the evenings. When she called him up shyly in the mornings to admit she was feeling lonely, he would invite her to his apartment behind the restaurant, make her tea and a potato, and encouraged her to nap on his single bed. They talked about cooking and art. They swapped knowledge. He never asked her about her first love affair. She was exempt from his interest. And she never pried because it was against her policy. Whenever he came close to her, she tipped her head, imperiling her wig, and smiled at him. She did not mind when he sat down with other friends or customers, although, sadly, the noise sometimes gave her a headache.

. . . something missing in Oliver, no that's not true, he's the most wonderful friend, admit it: Part of his niceness is that he appreciates one, at the same time, he appreciates nearly everyone, no, that's not true! yes it is! I agree, so that it is sort of a coincidence to have made friends with him and no more, funny,

I can't imagine him going bonkers for someone, a first love, I wonder whether he ever did. . . .

There was one person who knew how Oliver Weinstock's first relationship had ended, but that was Rudi Tonne, and he did not travel in Oliver Weinstock's circle. Still, Rudi Tonne was never too far from Oliver Weinstock. Twenty-odd years after their unfortunate encounter, Rudi Tonne had free access to Oliver Weinstock's mind and mood. He entered whenever he chose and stayed as long as he liked. Rudi Tonne was a memory.

Then one day a coincidence occurred, and Rudi Tonne turned up as a guest in his restaurant, giving Oliver Weinstock the opportunity to wrest control of his past.

2. A True Story Including Information About the Revolution, the Blues, a Timely Text, Hot and Cold

Rudi Tonne had made his first appearance during the winter holiday season when Oliver Weinstock turned fifteen and his parents had just divorced. His mother had taken all the girls to the West Side and left Oliver in the East Sixties with his father because, she said, "Women belong with women, men with men," although everyone knew she had a boyfriend.

His father fled their nearly empty apartment, taking Oliver to Saint Moritz. Because he was a generous, liberal man who feared his son might be bored with his elderly company, he allowed Oliver to invite his boyish fifteen-year-old girlfriend, Tina. Tina came without being impressed; she knew about first-class airplane seats and luxury hotels and divorce, and she fought her bad conscience about her privileges with bland acceptance of the status quo. She was, in short, a sensible girl. Neither she nor

Oliver had found any reason to be grown up. Sometimes they pretended to be in love with each other, and then they kissed in the manner of kittens exploring a new room. Otherwise they went skiing and bowling and swimming, they played in the snow, they ate, and they slept.

The days passed pleasantly. In the dining room their table was set for three, but generally by the time Oliver and Tina arrived in the morning, the third plate was full of crumbs and Mr. Weinstock was already on the ski slopes. He came home in the dark of the late afternoons, and occasionally Oliver caught a glimpse of him sitting in the lobby with a newspaper and a pot of tea, a tall, slender, elegant mourner at a funeral taking place within himself. They had three rooms next door to each other, but they rarely met up before dinner, a silent hour dreaded by them all.

Oliver thought about love, but he didn't yet know what it felt like. He knew only the mixture of fondness and hatred that he felt for his parents and sisters, and the pleasurable affection he felt for Tina and several other friends. Certainly he had no idea about emotional frenzy. His sexuality was onanistic. His first erotic encounter was with a children's book about animals, and it didn't occur until the very last page. A handsome illustration, a farewell gift to the young reader, depicted various wild animals. The zebra had his back to the reader. The lines of his backside swirled around and brought Oliver's eye—quite against his will! —to the cleavage of his buttocks. At fifteen, when Oliver was alone, that zebra's behind beckoned, warm and curved and irresistible. But for the past two weeks Oliver had rarely been alone. Now it was New Year's Eve, an occasion that generally proves to be the first and last disappointment of each year.

It was not on everyone's mind, of course, that this New Year's Eve was different because the Weinstock family was no longer together. The company was ignorant of this fact. The hotel guests assembled for a candlelit dinner in the dining room. A long buffet table of cold hors d'oeuvres had been set. The guests could help themselves to everything except lobster, which a young waiter, in a white hat and black-and-white checked suit, dispensed judiciously. The waiter was the only warm thing on the menu. He had white teeth and red lips and very fair hair, not only on his head but on his arms, which were visible when he extended his hand toward a patron, handing over the lobster. His torso, revealed between the wing doors of his jacket, was straight and hard. A white apron was tied around his middle. The wooden clogs on his feet added to his stature; he towered above the buffet table. More: he looked invulnerable, the picture of a hero, a victor. In short, he embodied what was good about the male sex.

As Oliver neared the golden fields of those forearms, glistening with dewdrops of sweat, something peculiar happened.

His emotions had always lined his being, like the inside of a coat. Now this relationship was turned inside out, so that his being lined his emotions. From one second to the next, Oliver Weinstock knew what romantic love was.

Oliver avoided the gaze of the buffetier, although he had an impression of deep blue eyes beneath a smooth, mysterious surface that on other people was merely a forehead. Oliver's own eyes were forced downward to the hands expertly handling a lobster tail. As one hand reached over to the young guest's plate, a thumb brushed his thumb.

Oliver had the sensation, as he explained it to himself later, that "everything slipped."

With his hand trembling so violently that he could hardly hold his plate, he retreated to his father and Tina. Instead of taking his seat next to Tina, with his back to the buffet table, he sat next to his father. Peering past the savage bonfire of the candles and the kaleidoscopic wineglasses, he could see the buffetier, and every glimpse of him was fixed forever on the meticulous, mechanical film plate of his brain. He wolfed the lobster tail, forgot to use his napkin, and raced to the buffet table for seconds. The buffetier nodded in acknowledgment, while his eyes stayed hooked into Oliver's eyes. Again, passing the lobster tail over the table, their hands brushed.

"It is democracy, all men are created equal, and we must drink with the servants!" cried Oliver upon returning to his place.

"Those aren't servants," remarked Tina in the interest of precision. "Servants do everything for you. These here set the tables and pass the lobster."

"Employees," agreed Mr. Weinstock, whose tongue had been loosened by two glasses of wine.

"Let us invite the employees for a drink!" continued Oliver. In the background, the kitchen personnel were clearing the buffet table. Before his father could protest, Oliver poured himself a glass of white wine and drained it in one gulp as the buffet table was carried out of the dining room. Could this be all? wondered the boy desperately.

Now the main meal began its long, odious course. On the menu was pigeon roulade—the bones of the bird were removed, and then the meat was beaten until tender and rolled around gherkins and tiny onions. This was served with truffle sauce and alpine potatoes whose tops had been lopped off, their contents scraped out, mashed with leeks and bacon, and returned to their jackets. Silence at the Weinstock table. The buffetier had disappeared into the kitchen, where Oliver occasionally glimpsed his head through the round windows of the swinging door. He felt his father's elbow moving up and down, up and down next to him. "Let us invite the employees for a drink, or dessert, or something," Oliver repeated. "There's room at our table."

"No there's not," observed the sensible Tina. The table next to them happened to be empty. "We'll push the tables together," insisted Oliver.

Before his father could object, Oliver stood up and moved the furniture. The maître d'hôtel appeared, alarmed. Oliver Weinstock looked at him disdainfully. "We're having guests," he said. Then he turned around and headed toward the kitchen. He had never been in a restaurant kitchen, but then he was rarely in his own kitchen at home.

"Come drink to the new year!" he cried in English, bursting through the swinging doors, finding himself in a hot fog amid huge, clanging kitchen machines, human figures gliding about in the background. The staff had been emptying bottles all evening and were in a state of advanced joviality. The manager, scurrying in from behind, held back his objections and shrugged. It was New Year's Eve, after all.

A group of men who did not have family and were not in a hurry to get home followed Oliver back to the table. Other guests staggered over, full of drunken enthusiasm, and began pushing tables together until the entire company was united. Oliver managed to make it seem like a coincidence as he slipped into the seat, many chairs down from his father and Tina, next to the buffetier. It proved no easier for Oliver to look at him close up: The smooth walls of his face, the glittering eyes caged behind the bars of their dark lashes, the adornment of blond eyebrows and pretty features seemed to the boy of an eerie perfection that deflected one's gaze; all he could do was sit in a silence he himself judged stupid, dazed by his own admiration.

The buffetier did not object. His manner was modest, touchingly friendly, naive, like a beautiful child who is unaware of the impression he makes. When Oliver finally summoned the strength to ask him "Who are you?" he replied, "The sauce cook," and it was only when, after another round of drinks, the guests exchanged names that his was revealed as Rudi Tonne.

Rudi Tonne was what Mr. Weinstock called "a born helper." He stood up when someone's glass was empty and refilled it. He passed the bread and helped the more drunken members of the party decide which cheese they wanted. When midnight came he sat down again. And as the entire company toasted the new year, he smiled apologetically, so it seemed to his young admirer, at nothing in particular.

Oliver Weinstock's own memories of this occasion, sharply focused up to this point, now become vague. There was a wind in his head. Bits of conversation about food and snow conditions turned around in this blinding torrent. Then the wind stopped. Memory resumed. He now knew that Rudi Tonne was twenty-three years old, that he made dessert sauces, and that he was a fine skier. *Was so ein Mann nicht alles alles kann!*

Beneath the table, Oliver moved his foot next to Rudi Tonne's white clog. He slipped his foot out of his shoe and onto the clog, and then Rudi Tonne slipped his foot out of his clog and laid it down on top of Oliver's foot.

At some point Oliver withdrew his foot, put his loafer back on and stood up, his chair giving a howl. At once Rudi Tonne's chair gave an answering howl as he stood up too, and they both went, with a haste normal during a time of heavy drinking, to the men's room.

It was a solemn occasion. They assumed their positions in front of the pissoirs, unzipped and unbuttoned their clothes, and revealed themselves, as has been done, is done, and will be done. "A fact," Oliver Weinstock mumbled. "The average man spends three months and two weeks of his life urinating. I read that once." And then he blushed, because he was unable to urinate for a certain visible reason—overwhelming feeling impaired his capacity. Nothing to laugh about in the hush of the men's room. As he stood at the sink to wash his hands as one has been taught to do, Rudi came up from behind and embraced him.

Without speaking, they left the building through a side door and sank down together into the nearest snowbank. They kissed, rolling over and over in the snow, kisses that were not bumbling explorations but statements and declarations. After a while Rudi Tonne stood up and pulled the younger boy after him. "When everyone's asleep, come to me," he said in the same tone of voice that he recommended a particular cheese.

When Oliver returned to the table, he did not sit down again but hovered behind his chair, yawning and looking at his watch. "I have to go to bed this minute," he said. Tina, who had been forced by Oliver's absence to make chitchat with the dour Mr. Weinstock, sprang up and trotted huffily to the elevator. The Weinstocks went to their adjoining rooms, and although it was customary for the father to leave the youngsters to their good-night kiss outside Tina's door, Tina was the first to disappear this evening; Mr. Weinstock and his son together. They peered at each other through the gloom of their different obsessions and

Mr. Weinstock said, "Happy New Year, kid," and Oliver said, "You too, Dad," and then their doors closed behind them.

It would be a good while before the help finished cleaning the kitchen and could retire for the night. He had to wait. He sat on the edge of the bed and waited, an easy target for fear and impatience. Finally he snatched a page of hotel stationery. There was one way of speaking to Rudi Tonne now, even if it was one-sided conversation: He could write to him. But what did he have to say? Over and over he mulled the possibilities. Finally he wrote the truth:

"I love you."

He folded the piece of paper and placed it inside his breast pocket. Then he set off on his rendezvous.

The night was dark and calm now, the snowbanks lit the way to the staff quarters, a barracks at the far side of the hotel property, where the landscaping ended and wilderness began. The entrance to these quarters lay on the dark back side of the barracks, which was perched on the edge of a steep, wooded incline. The tipsy visitor had to balance along this edge looking for the door. Inside it was even darker. A narrow, cheaply carpeted corridor had a dozen doors along one side, radiators and windows on the other. One door was standing slightly ajar. Without questioning it, Oliver entered. He kept congratulating himself, This is life at last!

The room was tiny; a pair of skis stood up against the wall, and boots and shoes and items of clothing lay underfoot. Rudi Tonne lay waiting in bed, fully alert, his eyes gleaming, his arms spread to receive his guest. Oliver Weinstock's memory generally digressed at this point.

He went back and savored his impressions of Rudi Tonne, and

his own innocent longing for him, which seemed unique and simple and pre-ordained. In those few hours that had passed since he had first fallen in love, Oliver had managed to think about the significance of it. He had a theory: Fate was a stream that had been carrying him, a bobbing passive vessel, toward Rudi. He had another theory: His whole life had been set up just to house his affection for Rudi. These thoughts were part of Oliver Weinstock's memory. Then they returned him to Rudi's arms.

Oliver was lying on his back in Rudi's bed, suddenly rather shy, waiting for instructions from the older man, when Rudi rolled over and sat astride Oliver's chest. He said, "Serve me," his voice severe, demanding. Before Oliver had a chance to fathom this request, Rudi grasped his head between his beautiful hands, wrenching it forward, and then he rammed an enormous truncheonlike thing into Oliver's mouth. He withdrew this briefly, only to slam it back in again. When Oliver struggled, gagging and choking, Rudi increased the rate and the pressure of his attack. Just as the poor boy thought he would suffocate, Rudi pulled back his dreadful weapon and something wet spurted over Oliver's face.

In the darkness, Rudi Tonne wiped Oliver's chin carefully with his sweaty undershirt and said in a fatherly voice, "I think you better go home now." Oliver protested, grasping for some sort of salvation, that he could stay the night, but Rudi Tonne said, "Oh no. They mustn't find you here. Besides," he said, his voice proud, "I'm getting married next week. My girlfriend is coming here and we're flying to Majorca together. Charter flight."

3. Ashes to Ashes: Oliver Weinstock's Confessions
Turn to Gossip

On a bitterly cold midwinter afternoon twenty years later, the entire staff was on hand when a man rang up and asked to reserve a table for two, giving his name as Tonne. They saw Oliver Weinstock lose his composure, stand up, cry, "Oh dear, oh dear," and travel in circles around the restaurant.

"There are a lot of people in the world named Tonne," he said, reaching the door of the kitchen.

"I don't know anyone of that name," said the cook.

"Do we have lobster on the menu?" asked Oliver Weinstock, and wandered off again.

"Lobster!" Frau Bussjäger called after him, holding her wig in place. "Of course not!"

"Buy some," said Oliver Weinstock. "We'll have lobster tail tonight. And pigeon roulade." And then he began to shake and shiver, as he yanked out a chair from a set place and plummeted down into it, the frayed page he always carried in the breast pocket of his suit fluttering between his fingers. He stared at the pale remnants of the three words written there, paying frantic attention to the details of each letter. When he had written it, when the pen tip held by his hand had touched the page, coincidence was about to maul him, but he didn't know it.

"You can't alter a memory the way you redo a house," he said. "You can't build on it, or repaint it, or use it as a garden shed if it's a palace. And you cannot tear it down."

The staff stood in the kitchen doorway watching him. They shook their heads and went back to work. Frau Bussjäger launched herself on a shopping expedition. Anything for Herr Weinstock. When she returned, he joined her in the kitchen, preparing the pigeon roulade himself.

. . . odd . . . very odd . . . some are odder than others. . . . some are driven to odd pleasures, odd beyond one's imagination and therefore disturbing, one shrugs their oddness off. . . .

Punctually at eight, a tall, heavyset man appeared and asked for the table he had reserved. "Appeared" does not convey his manner of arriving. Rudi Tonne walked with the help of metal crutches that looked like they were manacled to his forearms. His face was marked by the pleasant messiness that middle age often leaves on small-featured faces; his blue eyes, his nose and mouth, lay in warm, unmade beds of flesh, and his gray hair had a slight yellow tint, like a stain that would not wash out. Oliver Weinstock, standing at the bar, watching the door, recognized him at once. "Herr Tonne?" he asked. And he extended his hands to help him remove his coat. Herr Tonne followed Oliver to his table, his crutches tapping, his feet dragging. "I recommend the lobster tail," said the host.

"Never touch the stuff," replied Herr Tonne. "But pigeon roulade—I don't think I've ever had that."

"I recommend it," insisted Oliver Weinstock. "You reserved for two?" He helped his guest sit down and propped his crutches against the next chair. "Just one. I don't take anyone along on business trips," he replied.

"What kind of business, sir?" asked the host, rubbing his ice-cold hands.

"Oh, this and that," said the guest. "Export, import. Live in Bern, but I travel a lot. Even on crutches. I'll be off them soon. Fractured my legs in six places. Skiing accident. The slope was a pigsty, dirt and ice. I had plaster up to my waist. It's alright now. And I'm used to eating alone in restaurants." And he looked curiously at Oliver Weinstock. "You're American. They don't know anything about food."

"That guest," chafed Frau Bussjäger, running in and out of the kitchen, where Oliver Weinstock was helping the cleaner with the floor. "He orders a little of everything." She returned to report, "He's barely tasted any of it." In her opinion, the guest was also drinking a great deal. Hopefully he planned to pay. He seemed to have no intention of finishing and leaving. At closing time, Rudi Tonne was still sitting there, turning a spoon through a dish of sherbet. The cook and his assistant had already left. "I'll stay with him," said Oliver Weinstock to the others. "You can go home." Frau Bussjäger was hurt to the quick. She obeyed, coolly registering his ability to wound her.

"A grappa on the house!" Oliver Weinstock said as he heard

the restaurant door slam shut. He pulled up a chair to join his guest. "You're not married?" he asked.

Rudi Tonne frowned and nodded his head. "Of course I'm married," he said in a grumpy voice, accepting the grappa, not recognizing the first soft sounds of mental intrusion.

"I am not," said Oliver Weinstock.

He shrugged. "You'll have your good reasons."

"Indeed, I do," said Oliver Weinstock. "I have the reason of a prior engagement."

Rudi Tonne smiled pleasantly. "That's a good one." He tipped his glass; the grappa lapped through his lips. He smacked them. They were still wet, glistening, as he spoke.

"My wife is named Martha. She works in a travel agency part time. Gets free tickets for us. Would you like to see pictures of her? My children?" He leaned forward, removed his wallet. There lay two girls and a boy in their anonymous baby versions. He said their names, their current ages. Then a photo of a couple in wedding outfits, in profile, slim, similar, toasting each other.

"I'm telling you, I am very happily married. There is such a thing." He spoke freely, his words were not sticky with after-thought. "We have a nice house. Good neighbors. The garden is a little small, but"—he shrugged—"you can't have everything."

"Have you never betrayed her?" asked Oliver Weinstock, pouring his guest another grappa. He looked at his own full glass.

"Never," said Rudi Tonne. "Why should I?" He put his hand around the glass, holding himself steady.

"Some men are afraid of disease," said Oliver Weinstock gaily. "They make very loyal husbands. *Prosit!*" He wanted to toast to that.

Rudi Tonne's hand stayed, curled in a fist around his glass. He shook his head as if he had not understood, and then he said, "I was restless once, I had no control over my feelings. I didn't enjoy it. Curiosity is a kind of untidiness of your mind."

"You cured yourself?" asked Oliver Weinstock. *"Kuriert vom Krimskrams der Imagination?"*

His guest closed his lips, unsure of what to say. He was not used to conversation that bore one off into uncharted waters. He did not want to be impolite. "I'm an excellent husband," he said with finality. "I have never heard my wife complain. My children love me. It is my intention to be happy. This skiing accident —a little thing. It doesn't scare me. I find marriage satisfactory. I mean, why not? Once you have made a decision, you should stick to it! I have never looked at another woman, never; I have never even considered divorce."

"Divorce is a way of giving one's marriage a significance," Oliver Weinstock said, "that it otherwise lacks. Big feelings again. But of course you're right. It doesn't change anything, a divorce." He drank to emphasize that. His guest followed suit. Oliver Weinstock refilled the glasses.

"My parents were happily married in New York. They had friends, a couple named Peters. Mrs. Peters was the fragile, sad one, Mr. Peters the strong, happy-go-lucky one. He took care of everything; as a teacher, he had time on his hands. His delicate wife dominated him, with intolerant opinions and, in a pinch, with some devastating illness that no doctor could prove. A real lady. She was always reading Goethe's *Faust*. Then Mr. Peters began to notice my mother. My mother was the opposite of Mrs. Peters. She was strong, tolerant, energetic, a Brooklyn chatterbox. She took the stairs three at a time and she preferred being in a good mood. She was married to my father, of course, a dedicated businessman who never had any time for her. With relief, Mr. Peters fell in love with Mrs. Weinstock, and Mrs. Weinstock fell in love with Mr. Peters. He left his wife, she left her husband.

"After a while, Mr. Peters was always ill, always complaining, and ever more intolerant and domineering. To get away from him, my mother opened a business and never had any time. Mr. Peters talked about Faust while the former Mrs. Weinstock talked about profit margins and taxes. They reenacted their first marriages in their second marriages. Why? You tell me, please. You're married. It's different with pure sex, of course. That doesn't leave much of a trace, does it?"

"I would like the bill, please," said Rudi Tonne, fumbling for his crutches. The handles had hooked over the top of the neighboring chair. Oliver Weinstock did not help him untangle them. He handed him his glass of grappa.

"Some prefer passive sex," he was saying with a frown. "Service. Some prefer to serve. I was in a production of *Salomé* in New York. During the second intermission, I wanted to go for a walk outside the opera house. A man was leaving ahead of me. Someone tall, sturdy. A summer night. On the stairs, he turned around and glanced at me. His look was a fusillade. I stayed a few meters behind him on the sidewalk, and when he veered off into a bush, I followed him. He was waiting for me. A huge Adam's apple. And a long body, too long for his legs. The red hair on his head upright like a cock's comb. He reached for my head and pushed it down where he wanted it. I still remember the full moon that was watching though the bushes. It was a very simple job, and I was so happy and at the same time so sad to oblige him. It reminded me of something, yes, it did remind me of something. When he was satisfied, he packed himself up again and without even saying good-bye, he ducked out of the bushes, leaving me behind, drenched with moonlight.''

"I must go now," said Rudi Tonne, pushing his grappa glass aside, pulling out his wallet, his face cramped with dislike. He dropped a number of large bills onto the table and said, "This will cover everything, I'm sure." He managed to disengage one crutch and he stood up with that, grimacing as he put his weight on his legs. He wrestled with the other crutch. "I'll get your coat," offered Oliver Weinstock.

He had put on his own coat when he returned with the luxurious cashmere garment that belonged to his guest. He stood behind Herr Tonne and guided his arms into the sleeves, saying, "I was only trying to take my mind off things. And someone saw us. Someone saw us and I was still sitting there in the bushes, recovering, when the police came. It turned out that the man was young, underage. He said I had taken the initiative. Forced him.''

Rudi Tonne and Oliver Weinstock were standing in the doorway of the restaurant, staring out at the street. A peculiar sight: The moonlight lay splashed on the sidewalk. It had drizzled earlier in the evening and then the temperature had dropped. The street looked like a frozen river. Rudi Tonne put his crutches down carefully and they slid. He looked at the ground with fear. The ground is the enemy of the man with bad legs. "My hotel is just down the street," he mumbled unwillingly.

Oliver Weinstock said, "I will help you there." He locked the door from outside and slid his hand under the injured man's arm, supporting him, like a vise. The crutches rattled on his forearms.

"I was just looking for a souvenir, though. The memory of him. Sometimes a new experience alleviates an old mental wound. Sometimes it presses on it, causing pain. You never know in advance how something will affect an old memory. And it turns out that new memories are wasted on me. I can't feel them, somehow. There are some injuries so painful that they destroy all the nerves."

Rudi Tonne had no choice but to accept Oliver Weinstock's help. At first he tried to keep the contact to a minimum. But when he lost his footing and began to slide on the ice, panic and common sense prevailed, and he dropped himself into his companion's arms. Oliver Weinstock held the taller, heavier man and helped him upright again, murmuring reassurances.

At once the wind broke in a wave over them. Rudi Tonne was frightened. He did not want to let go of Oliver Weinstock. He practically hung in his arms. And Oliver Weinstock propped him upright, keeping one hand on his lower back and the other on his hip, to steady him. They proceeded like that. "Once, after I left New York, in Venice," chatted Oliver Weinstock, "I had a family man, in a camel fur coat, fifty years old, a comfy old gent, oh, he was very happy with me. He kneeled in front of me between the souvenir stalls at Saint Marco's, at night in wintry Venice. He pushed his round little bald head into my groin, and the streetlights were reflected in his pate. Great service. Such enthusiasm. It was really infectious. I wanted to be generous and free with him, so I traded places. He hadn't expected that. In his cotton long johns, he had himself all trussed up with strings. I lit a match, so I could see what I was doing, and pulled at the strings, which gave him great pleasure. Afterward he wanted to show his appreciation, and his wallet suddenly appeared in his hand, a buffed leather wallet. But before he could pull out some money, I stuffed a bill into it. Imagine his joy at this small side income. He said, 'Come to my drugstore at the corner of Saint

Marco, you can have anything you like.' But there was nothing I wanted, and I left Venice."

The wind battered them, sprayed snow, and sent Rudi Tonne's coat flying open. Oliver Weinstock stopped, and while Rudi Tonne leaned on his shoulder, he began to button his coat shut for him, chatting amiably.

"My family didn't want me to leave America. But I was a shocking embarrassment to them. The first time I was fifteen. Then I picked up a sexual disease in my mouth. I wouldn't say from whom. I am not Oliver Weinstock, you know. I am Gretchen." He finished the last button and said, "It's a fact."

Rudi Tonne moved his legs stiffly, as though he was wading through deep water. "A man toyed with me," Oliver Weinstock continued in a soothing tone of voice. "Yes, he did." He saw that his companion wasn't listening and added, "You have a beautiful coat, by the way."

"Thank you," he grunted, looking at the ground, working to keep his balance.

"The man Gretchen loved didn't have a pact with the devil, he had a deal with coincidence. He could do anything he wanted. With his Gretchen. She ran after him. And after she carried his disease in her mouth, the family said: Feh! Disgusting! Where did you buy that coat, Herr Tonne?"

"In Zurich. If you need a winter coat—Zurich. Not Bern."

"Zurich, thank you. My story goes on. When Gretchen was arrested, that was it. It was just for one night but what a night. And then there were charges against her. She left. She went to Germany. She still wasn't exactly free to move around, though."

Rudi Tonne was panting with exertion, his breath swirled around them. His face looked wet; he was sweating.

"Depending on the individual, the past is either a drainhole or a jailhouse. I think of Gretchen as being under arrest for over twenty years. Her Faust was not an intellectual—he was a trivial magician. He could cast spells."

Rudi Tonne stared at the light of the entrance hall up the street, as if his gaze could pull him there.

"Did you know we've met before?" asked Oliver Weinstock.

It seemed a question of luck to Rudi Tonne whether he would ever make that doorway. He tried to walk faster, and skidded, embracing Oliver Weinstock's shoulders and waist, pressing his head against Oliver's chest, the crutches dangling.

Rudi Tonne drew back and managed on his own again.

"Forgive me for talking nonsense," said Oliver Weinstock sincerely. "It doesn't fit, not at all. You're the one in shackles, and I'm helping you. In the final scene, coincidence turns the tables. All these years thinking of myself as Gretchen!" He was laughing. "Forgive me! Besides, there's a happy ending. Gretchen gets resurrected, and she has her Faust, after he dies. Oh dear, forgive me, I've been talking such nonsense to my dinner guest."

"It's fine, it's fine," said Rudi Tonne, accepting the apology as a return to normalcy. "I don't know what you're talking about anyway," he added in a small-talk sort of voice, not really paying attention, wanting to distract himself from the danger, wanting to be in his hotel room. "Who's Faust? I don't know him. Gretchen is a girl's name."

They didn't speak anymore. When they reached the doorway of the hotel, Rudi Tonne must have had an attack of gratitude. He said, "Come inside for a drink, won't you? You've brought me this far."

"The hotel bar will be closed, but your minibar will be open," agreed Oliver Weinstock. "I have a small text that I wrote down for you once, and I've been carrying it around for more than twenty years, but I don't think I will show it to you, no, it's very short, I may just throw it away. But I'll tell you some of my theories about love and coincidence." He had his matches in his hand already.

Frau Bussjäger had ample reason to reflect on this guest, Rudi Tonne. It was a peculiar night. So cold and yet so hot. There was a fire in the hotel down the street, and several guests, old or incapacitated and unable to escape, were killed. Anonymous death upset her particularly because it stimulated her imagination. She had wanted to ask Oliver Weinstock whether he had seen the fire, but the very next day Oliver Weinstock called her at home and declared the restaurant closed. He left abruptly for New York and came back only once, to finalize the sale of the premises. He had opened a restaurant in Manhattan, he said, and he was planning to get rich. He asked Frau Bussjäger to join him, but she was angry and proud and had already found another job. She had had a shock, cleaning up the restaurant the day after the fire. She had come across a note in the garbage. It was just asking to be read, cut up into a dozen little pieces. She had fished them all up out of the trash, along with a lot of food scraps. She had experience.

Her first great disappointment in love had come from a wastebasket. Her fiancé had left just such a pile of snippets in the bin under his desk. She had gone to see him, and he was not home. Where was he? She had taken out the bits and put them together like a puzzle—it had been a nightmarish amount of work—and had then read the repaired page. It was a passionate letter to his little sister. She had married him anyway but never ever forgiven him.

Looking at the sodden bits of paper on the morning after the fire, she told herself that the truth wants to be known. She wept and went to work. A lot of effort for only three words, as it happened.

She did not keep the results to herself. From her new position in another restaurant, she released them into the grapevine, where, in the absence of their owner, they luxuriated, grew, sprouting the loveliest gossip about love that had been heard in the city for a long time.

. . . he left a love letter to Frau Bussjäger, yes, to Frau Bussjäger the old manageress, yes, that's it, that's his thing, weird, she'd turned him down and then he closed up the shop, he sent her the letter, funny what breaks one man's heart, wouldn't affect mine, what a shame there's scarcely anyone really nice left now. . . .

An

Innocent

Vacation

I spent the Kingdom of Libya's last sundown occupying a park bench in front of King Idris's palace in Tripoli. The palace gates stood open and unguarded, and I knew how pleasant the grass by the rose bushes would be when I finally unrolled my sleeping bag there. The bench was on a quay that ran along the harbor where men strolled in groups. I liked the fact that in public Arab society was exclusively male because this supported my feeling that I was a man too. I was seventeen years old, female, penniless, and well traveled. I had been on the road all summer, and now it was autumn. The simplicity of my journey seemed to generate its momentum.

It had been my parents' idea to send me overseas from New York. They believed that the long American school holidays were the cause of juvenile delinquency. In 1968 I had been infected by a girlfriend at an arts and crafts course downtown with an alarming rebelliousness they feared would inflame in the heat of the 1969 summer. Promptly after the semester ended they sent me to farming relatives in Austria, where the weather was cool, the farmyard animals emotionally involving, and the household chores exhausting. After flying to Frankfurt, however, the leg of the flight to Salzburg seemed redundant to me; I cashed in the ticket and headed for a youth hostel. There I met an American who had been to Chicago in 1968. He said, "The kids are going east this year." That set my itinerary. I hitchhiked east—if I had any unpleasant experiences I did not notice them—until I reached a place where the kids talked only about the price of hashish (Tehran); I did not enjoy hallucinating, so I went west again, until my money ran out (Venice). After I sold my army surplus knapsack and all of its contents at a flea market, I was left with one finest quality goosedown sleeping bag from Macy's, good to minus forty degrees, and the Indian shift from West Fourth Street, with a blue-and-white bunny rabbit motif, that I was wearing at the time of the sale. The dress was square-shaped and crowded with these bunnies, so that the first words Charles said to me were, "I see you're traveling by hutch."

Charles was an Englishman I met in Venice. He treated me as no more or less than the traveling companion he had sought on a hostel bulletin board. Charles was garrulous and secretive, he was en route from Oxford to Alexandria with only a leather handbag that contained a copy of Durrell's *Alexandria Quartet* and a thick, tattered manuscript that he referred to as his first novel. His vacation was even longer than mine, so he was going to work his way across the Mediterranean as a deckhand on a ship and then hitchhike to Egypt. He wanted company. This sounded better to me than returning to the eleventh grade at a private school in Manhattan. That is how I came to be in Tripoli on the twentieth of September, 1969, waiting for darkness to obscure the moment I retired to bed in His Majesty's gardens.

At school I had never realized what an idyllic place the world was. It was peopled with adults, to be sure, but if one wasn't culturally related to them, they were an amiable, generous lot. I assumed generosity motivated a guard at the Tunisian-Libyan border to invite us in for the evening at the border station. The border guards were irritable with other travelers. For some reason, they did not want to let anyone into Libya. They even turned away a busload of Italian tourists with valid visas. But we were singled out for special treatment. "You have nowhere to sleep?" a guard asked us solicitously. He proved to be the captain of the unit. He personally escorted us through the dining room, where we loaded metal plates with couscous and fried fish, and then when we had eaten the multiple helpings he urged on us, he showed us to a dormitory with a dozen camp beds. It smelled ghastly in there, after a few hours, of digesting onions.

At some hour of the night, the following incident occurred: A figure I recognized as our friend stumbled, falling on top of me. I tried to help him to his feet but he seemed incapable of regaining his balance, falling back down on top of me and somehow becoming tangled up inside my blanket. Finally, alarmed for him, I cried for help. Inexplicably, he fled, a dark stick figure leaping past the rows of beds with their snoring guards until he was out the door.

The next morning no one paid attention to us. The border was still closed, but the driver of a Mercedes from Istanbul entered after waving a fistful of dollar bills. He would have to pass through Tripoli, and he took us along. His wife was English. She sat in the rear with us, and as we watched the flat back of her husband's head, she complained in whispers how he mistreated her, how he didn't permit her to speak, how he forced her to wear unfashionable Arab clothing, and worse, how once a year he circumnavigated the Mediterranean by road only to show off his car to the family in Cairo, instead of flying or taking the ferry from Istanbul. "When I was his secretary in London, I loved him," she assured us. Her husband dropped us off at the harbor front of Tripoli where the quay began. Immediately a melon vendor there who had admired the Mercedes handed us a melon. We cracked the melon on the curbstone and ate it, squatting by the roadside. I wiped the melon juice from my hands onto my dress and the fabric became stiff. I began to notice the heat.

The quay continued for miles, with the harbor on one side and small shops, palm trees, and low, modern houses on the other. After we had walked for a long way and this scenery had not altered at all, Charles began to scowl. He said, "There is something unpleasant about this country. I can't put my finger on it yet."

Charles squinted at the sea and rubbed his pale blue eyes. He was very tall and straight without being athletic, he had fine features and curly blond hair without my finding him particularly handsome, he was well educated without being erudite, good-natured without being obnoxious. It was in Tripoli that I realized he could have a bad mood. "I'm hot and sticky, damn those melons, damn those Arabs and their unquenchable generosity. You can never say no, can you?"

"Yes I can, sure I can," I promised him.

"You're so American," he accused me.

"Let's go swimming in the harbor," I answered soothingly.

"You're so naive."

I blushed. I had told him in Venice when we were discussing our trip together that I was deeply in love with a boy back home whose name I invented, Peter Baxter. As we were hitchhiking to the ferry in Naples I made sure to mention this phantom regularly: "I must write Peter," "I do wonder what Peter is doing at college." I even dropped Peter a postcard before boarding the ferry; after that I forgot about Peter, and I hadn't spoken about him in a month. Charles never mentioned any girl either, he never talked about his friends or family. I simply presumed there was no one in his life of the same importance as his traveling companion.

He followed me down a flight of stairs that led from the quay to the sea, where small boats and larger yachts were moored. We went into the water with our clothes on, swam around to look at the most luxurious ships, chased each other through the water. When Charles caught me, he patted my shoulder and arm and remarked, "Look how beautiful your skin is here." I agreed. My skin was very brown and smooth.

Afterward we climbed back to the quay and continued our walk in wet clothes that soon dried. We had reached a place where the dirty modern buildings gave way to gardens with a violet sensuousness of roses and rhododendron. Set back in a grove stood a simple but vast white building.

"The king's palace, you can't come in," said a guard in Italian. "Or do you speak English?" He was going to show off. "Here the king lives. But our good king is not here now, Good King Idris. He went out, to Cyprus, because he is sick." He turned away and said, "Old and sick but good. Ten years I work for him." He had outgrown his prime in Idris's service. He had no front teeth but a smart gray-green uniform and a bright Uzi gun.

"So we can sleep here, if he's not there," I said.

The guard laughed incredulously. "Sleep in here!" He didn't want to talk to us anymore. He stood at attention. We peered around him into Idris's paradise, and we saw that the roses were wilting: The ground next to the rose bushes was covered with red and black petals. Charles pointed, there. We'll sleep there. The guard was still introspective. Then he jerked his head as a communication. He muttered, "I leave at ten. Two minutes there is no one. Then you can go in."

We waited on the park bench near the gate and Charles observed, "The citizens look pecunious." He delivered a commentary, as he always did when we reached a new place.

"If you judge Tripoli by its smells, then it consists of roses and gasoline, sea and onions."

"The harbor is quite lovely, I must admit, even if it has no shape. Harbors should be formed by the land into a rounding, whereas this just began somewhere with a few moored dingies, and that is how it probably ends on the other side of town. But the water is royal blue, the yachts here are exquisite, and even the sun is plumper and oilier than in Tunisia. Like a fried yolk. I am getting hungry. We better do something for food soon."

Charles began to make eye contact with passing strangers in a way that indicated friendly interest. I kept a bright American smile on my face as a backdrop.

The Libyans were less responsive than the Tunisians. A few nodded and spoke the English words they knew, "hello, good-bye" or "New York, Texas, Apollo." One man said "Howdy." And then a party of three in suits slowed as they passed us, responded to our smiles, and one remarked, "Isn't Tripoli beautiful?"

"One of the most beautiful cities I have ever seen in my long travels," Charles returned. The three stood around us, careful not to block the view. The man who had addressed us ordered his companions to buy us lemonade from a peddler. The sun had hit the horizon of the Mediterranean and was spilling yellow light everywhere. We watched the others gliding through the sunset holding glasses of lemonade.

"Americans are good, Russians are bad," our host made a toast. He was the houseboy of an American oil executive. He was dressed like an executive himself, with a freshly pressed suit. His face looked rather pinched for his age and he smelled of after-shave. He asked us about ourselves—where we came from, how we were traveling—and translated extensively for his friends, who could understand no English at all. They pressed close to us, eager to watch us speak. How old were we? What were our names? Were we married?

"We would like to invite you to dinner," said the elegant houseboy. His name was Jeff. "We are going to the finest restaurant in Tripoli." He had his own Fiat in which to take us.

The Fiat was small and immaculate, Jeff's pride in it huge. Following his example we cleaned our feet and brushed off our sleeves and shoulders before crawling into the back, his friends squeezing into the front. Large American and small Italian cars skirmished on a main road, the conflict ending suddenly when the main road turned into a sand dune. We parked there among a dozen other cars lining a garishly lit construction with a neon sign: AMERICAN DESERT BAR AND RESTAURANT.

"My boss comes here when he wants a really American steak," said Jeff in a voice pitched high with excitement. He ordered steaks and Miller High Life. His friends seemed uncomfortable; they ate hurriedly and did not look around. But they concentrated on Charles's conversation. He was telling them things about himself I did not know: that his father was a businessman, that his family house had two stories and a garden, that he played rugby, that they ate fish and fried potatoes in England as a sort of national craze. Charles was getting drunk and our hosts plied him with more beer. His face turned red and his brilliant posture degenerated into a slump. An Arabic dessert came in courses. By the time one of the sweet sauces suddenly ran back out of Charles's mouth, he had already begun a long slide downward into his red plastic seat and was wallowing on his side. Jeff propped him up. Everyone laughed sympathetically.

"Let us go for a drive into the desert," suggested Jeff to his friends. Up to this point he had not spoken to me once, and now he only glanced in my direction. "It is something everyone must see—the Sahara at night."

I was opposed to this. I was anxious not to miss the moment when the guard changed at Idris's palace gardens. I spoke for the first time that evening. I said, "Oh, thank you, but no thank you. We must get back. We are staying with friends near the palace." I was eager for Charles to return to normal.

But they insisted, and their enthusiasm was so great that I could not refuse. I was too well brought up to be impolite, and they were after all adults. The three Libyans carried Charles out and stuffed him into the backseat of the Fiat, and I had no choice but to follow. He lay in my lap of blue and white bunnies, his head heavy and damp. It was dark outside. We drove a short distance in silence. The Sahara laps at the southern edge of Tripoli, running in streams into the streets, but Jeff wanted to drive far out where the sand was deep; for once, he wasn't going to pamper his car. The Fiat suffered loudly and then stalled. Jeff didn't care. "This is far enough," he said and rushed out. The others followed and began hustling me out too, pulling at my arm. They did not bother with Charles, so I took some time settling his head gently on the seat. I turned around into the monochrome scenery—the black sky and the dark sand. Nearby, something wailed.

"What's that?" I asked Jeff.

"Wild dogs," he answered carelessly. He was discussing something of great interest with the others. I realized by the way they were jerking their heads in my direction that they were in fact talking about me. They were arguing, and then Jeff pointed at a sand dune and they all nodded. Finally they looked at me directly.

"I have to get back to the palace now," I stated.

I found the very idea of unprotective behavior in an adult astonishing. Then, although I did not know what exactly a rape entailed, I became afraid. Charles slept noisily in the car. Instead of returning us to the palace, the three Libyans began to pull at my dress, ignoring the beautiful pattern of bunny rabbits on it. The dress was worn out from the saltwater and sun and it ripped over my left breast.

I was filled with indignity: How dare they!

There was a clap of thunder, flames shot up into the sky.

How repulsive and unjust!

The sky flickered with artillery, and over toward Idris's palace it turned white. Just as I burst into tears, Idris's gardens blew up.

My escorts became remorseful. They apologized in English and Arabic. This did not make the fireworks stop. They worked frantically to get Jeff's Fiat out of the sand and we jumped in and zigzagged through the chaos until we reached a sandy suburb of door-to-door bungalows with the great American vehicles parked in the front. This was the American sector of town. Jeff was home.

Jeff and I hauled Charles out and then he abandoned the car

to his friends. We laid him down in the living room on an American Pioneer sofa, where he kept sleeping. I became aware of a
waxy-skinned, balding fat man sitting at a coffee table listening
to a radio's baseball broadcast live from America. He addressed
Jeff, "Bring me a julep, will you." Then he turned to me. "Some
weather," he said. "Friends of Jeff's are friends of mine. Make
yourselves at home. He sick?"

Charles was indeed being sick, but it seemed to do him good
and Jeff cleaned him up. The cold water on his face made him
wake up; he sat up and looked acute. "It sounds like a football
game out there," he remarked.

"Baseball on the radio," said the American man. "Fred Bart,"
he continued, turning off the radio. "You sound English. My
mother was English, that's where I got the dark hair and blue
eyes. What's an Englishman doing in Tripoli? God that's noisy."

Jeff carried a tray of mint juleps, the glasses rattling because
his hands were shaking. "It's the Russians!"

"I will kill any Russian I see," cried Jeff. "America is a great
country. America is good. And Idris! Our good king. He went to
Cyprus. I hope he is safe." His sly face looked as if he was about
to cry.

I was tired. I unrolled my Arctic sleeping bag in a corner of the
rose-colored living room rug and went to sleep with the three
men talking around me.

The next morning, Jeff set a tray on the floor with milk, coffee, and cornflakes. He was extremely unfriendly.

"Don't ever call me Jeff," he said. "That was my boss's idea.
From now on my name is Mohammad again." A radio was apparently on in the kitchen. An Arabic voice cried out in long
paragraphs. This was followed by martial music. "We have been

saved from the evil Idris!'' Jeff explained. ''That old American puppet. The Americans are bad. The Russians are good. I should kill you, as an American. It is actually my duty.'' Then he returned to the kitchen.

I ate my cornflakes. I did not drink coffee because it was an adult drink. Charles was nowhere to be seen and it was mid-morning. Eventually I searched for him and found him sitting up, eating cornflakes in a king-size bed in the master bedroom. He complained of a headache. Fred Bart appeared in a terrycloth bathrobe and terrycloth slippers and remarked, ''You have to report to the embassy. They'll send you home—I gather you're under-age. There's been a revolution.'' He seemed unimpressed.

I spent the Republic of Libya's first day mending the rip in my dress, sewing the material over my left breast at an impossible angle because I did not dare to take the dress off. I wanted the situation to become familiar and simple again, the way it had been. But no one else shared my wish, not Jeff, who eventually stormed out of the house, leaving a martial voice ranting on the kitchen radio, nor Charles, who suddenly remarked, ''You and your innocence. How I've suffered!'', nor the anonymous men who had exploded my bed of roses.

Portrait

of a

Defection

Once upon a time, there was an East German mathematician named Herr Stein who did not feel East German. He had grown up in Shanghai, a tall, delicate, very pale Caucasian who spoke German with a tolling instead of a rolling of the *r*, and he spent most of his working hours in the West as an exchange scholar. He kept secret an apartment in Frankfurt and bank accounts in three countries, where he stored the money he made speculating illicitly on the stock exchange. He kept vague his relationship to several girlfriends in different Western cities. He depended on them for sex, transportation, and a hot meal, but he always called them after he had arrived in town, never before. His right to secrecy was the freedom he took the most seriously.

Aside from professors who invited him to meetings and lectures, only the "proper authorities" knew about his movements. Theirs was not an intimate relationship either, since they communicated only by letter or, in an emergency, by telephone. The authorities had underlings at the border wear their faces and hands for them. These agents of power were somber, even critical, but they never troubled Herr Stein and he was not afraid of them. He was much more afraid of his mother.

Herr Stein's mother lived in East Berlin, lived for the moment when her son finally came home, when she could welcome him with lamentations of gratitude and concern. Within minutes of his arrival, she would feed him. In East Berlin, there was no reason for Herr Stein not to share an apartment with his mother. Apartments were hard to come by, good housekeepers even harder. And Herr Stein found his mother neither more nor less frightening than any woman he had known, except that she alone had managed to rope him into living together. He loathed her for being too convenient to resist. But he knew convenience was an expensive commodity, on both sides of the wall.

The Western universities found in Herr Stein a convenience too. He fulfilled their emotional and political requirements for scientific exchange with the East. And, unlike some of his East German colleagues allowed to travel in the West, Herr Stein never voiced opinions about the internal affairs of the Bundesrepublik, the communal elections in Frankfurt did not interest him, nor did he comment on the chancellor's latest remarks about South Africa. In both East and West Germany, Herr Stein's keenness to make a good living was deemed proof of his political incorruptibility.

The East German government found Herr Stein most convenient of all. The universities where he lectured paid him in Western currency, which the East Germans could collect as taxes. If Herr Stein declared only half of what he earned and secreted the rest, the authorities were delighted to tax just half. Or if he claimed his entire cash payment had been stolen (as he did in principle every time he went to Italy), the government so desperately needed the Western currency that they didn't ask for details. They were relieved that Herr Stein kept his accounts of theft to a minimum. The East Germans considered Herr Stein a solid investment. He would always yield a percentage. He was deemed financially and politically predictable. In his files someone had noted Herr Stein's difficulties in forming relationships. His mother was his single most important emotional commitment: they were Frau and Herr Stein for eternity.

Yet he defected.

He had always known he would. For years he had let others suggest staying in the West. He had pretended their advice was out of the question, on the grounds of difficulty. His acquaintances from Western Europe liked to visit him in East Berlin, so it sometimes seemed to him, only in order to press him to defect. Actually they visited because they found Herr Stein exotic: an address behind the iron curtain. Exotic too was the newly tarred street of barren buildings where the wealthier residents of East Berlin lived in a style reminiscent of Western low-income housing. Exotic was the elevator that never functioned, the smell of urine in the halls, the tiny windows in the apartment, the heavy furniture and cheap carpeting. Most exotic of all was Herr Stein's mother, a woman of Oriental delicacy with her son's unusual deep-set eyes, his flat nose, his curly red hair. She always answered the door with a self-deprecating smile.

She retired immediately after showing a guest through two entrances to a living room kept much too full of chunky furniture. "If you're going to talk," she warned, nodding toward a monstrous Russian-label radio, "then don't forget to turn that on. Eavesdroppers, everywhere." She eavesdropped for a while

outside the closed door and then entered abruptly to serve coffee. The coffee was really coffee, not an ersatz made from chic-
ory, which meant that she had probably procured it in the West.
This was a disappointment to the visitors, despite being a relief,
and she explained, "When you are over sixty, as I am!, then you
can go Over There whenever you want. You just have to be back
Over Here by midnight. Otherwise"—she ran her index finger
across her throat—"or prison or I don't know what. I go over
there just to buy coffee. We're allowed to bring back one kilo
from each visit. I save it for visitors. The coffee here! Dreadful! If
I were young—if I were my son's age—I wouldn't put up with
it . . ." She jerked her head meaningfully at her son, who always looked away and hummed unmusically under his breath
while she talked.

She left the room and returned again suddenly with, "The
border police didn't ask where you were going? Spies everywhere!"

"Of course not," her guests reassured her. Naturally the border guards had asked, and they had told them where they were
going. It was much too much trouble to lie, and there could be
no harm at all in Herr Stein receiving a visit from another
scholar. Visitors either took spy stories seriously enough to stay
out of East Berlin altogether or they delighted in them. Most
found Frau Stein's paranoia exquisite.

When the company was not talking mathematics, Frau Stein
snapped on the radio herself and regaled them with complaints:
the harassment of reporting Herr Stein's expenditures, the endless queuing for shoddy goods, the malfunctioning elevator, the
spies. When her son stepped out of the room, she looked at his
empty chair and whispered, "He should defect! He has the

chance!'' She waited until he returned before continuing her monologue because she did not want him to miss a word of it. She had horror stories to tell, about the war and about the birth of her son. Her narrative style resembled that of a headline writer from a Western newspaper she had never read:

STARVING WOMAN BEARS CHILD IN MOUNTAIN TENT

MONGOLIAN TENT COLLAPSES AS WAR REFUGEE HAS BABY

BABY BORN IN −40°; GERMAN MOM HAS ONLY TIGER SKIN DIAPER

INNER MONGOLIA: GERMAN BABY BORN AT 5,000 METERS: THREE

POUNDS, FIVE OUNCES, LIVES!

Forty years later, Frau Stein's eyes welled up at the memory of her moment of glory. To be sure, she was easily moved to tears by the many sorrows that preoccupied her, including the bitter-sweetness of having a son and the death of her husband in the arms of a Chinese mistress preceding her return to Germany. On some days the tide of her tears ran so high that it flooded in public. The spies noted this with satisfaction. They knew the tears had nothing to do with socialism. They knew exactly her state of mind because she told everyone about it, not just guests behind closed doors with the radio blaring at home, but every person she met on the street, at the market. To the extent that she knew, she told them what her son was up to, so that the spies had an easy time keeping tabs on him through her prattle.

And finally the authorities had one absolutely solid guarantee that she—and therefore he—would never defect. The mathematician had bought his mother a silver fox coat in the West to assuage his conscience for neglecting her. He had smuggled it home by wearing it underneath his raincoat. He did not realize that this secret met with the full approval of the authorities, whose underlings reported his bulky appearance to headquarters before waving him through the control. The authorities knew that Frau Stein would never leave East Germany without that coat and that she would never dare smuggle it back over the border, either.

After she had told them of her woes, Frau Stein liked to show visitors the fur. She came into the living room with the coat buttoned up. She walked a few feet, turned around, walked another few feet, turned again with a flip of her head, and exclaimed what a wonderful son she had who truly cared. Her son hated her chatter. He would turn the radio up to top volume when she began, and by the time she was unbuttoning her silver fox coat, he would lose his temper and say, "Please, Mama, leave us with your stupid blather!"

And she would retreat tearfully in her half-open coat, taking the coffee cups.

"Poor Mama is such a child," he remarked to his visitors. "You see, I could never leave her here alone, and she would refuse to come West with me. She has no one else," he explained, waiting to be talked into leaving nonetheless. His visitors had the quaintest ideas about how to defect: you show up at an embassy without even a suitcase and shout, I'm defecting! They didn't realize the importance of having one's own familiar clothing, and they had no sense of timing. He pretended to listen carefully and skeptically to their advice until the topic of his defection had been exhausted. Afterward he lapsed into pubescent, off-color jokes, because he was basically uncommunicative and did not really know what to do with these visitors.

Certainly he could not complain to them about the condition that really moved him to defect: his mother.

All the while that he rejected the advice of his visitors to leave the repressive East, Herr Stein was stockpiling his worldly goods in the West. He did this with a patience and forethought they would have found inappropriate for such an event. He curried the friendship of several people he judged to be especially naive about politics. These were not the old ladies his mother knew who listened to the radio and were unbearably informed about everything going on in the world, but professionals—a political scientist, a psychologist, and a lawyer. He used to visit them casually and leave his suitcase "by accident," or his best over-coat, woolen scarves, ties, or fashionable shoes. The old women would have recognized what he was up to in a flash. But the professional friends, who assumed Herr Stein was low on money and clothes, only worried that he could freeze. "Put them aside for me, I'll collect them another time," he consoled them when they called him to report what they had found in their halls or guest rooms. The friends attributed a lot of his odd behavior admiringly to the nonmaterialism of the East, by which they didn't mean the Far East.

His defection was the final step in a long series of covert actions, this last one taking place in the broad daylight of the tabloids. The week before, Herr Stein had gone about his business as usual —he had slept and taken his meals at home in East Berlin, worked at the university during the day and seen no one. He had applied several weeks earlier for a one-day visa to West Berlin in order to consult certain books at a library there. The authorities had mailed him his passport and exit visa punctually and with-out question. He had suggested to his mother that she could accompany him across the border to visit one of her girlfriends;

he could give her a lift in the Volvo he had bought the year before for sixty thousand ostmarks. This purchase had depleted his East German savings, which he would no longer need in the West. He didn't think of himself as the type to defect in a Wartburg; it would look ridiculous.

The authorities had not found the Volvo troubling. They knew that driving a Wartburg in the West invited trouble. Certain West Berliners assumed that any East German allowed Over Here must be a government official. Herr Stein's car was attacked once while waiting at an intersection. Herr Stein was so law-abiding that he had not driven away (red light) and the vandals had enjoyed the full thirty seconds it took the light to change to smash three windows, shouting, "Tell this to Honecker!" The repairs had taken weeks. Herr Stein's Volvo was understandable and a familiar sight at the border crossing, so he could drive comfortably to his defection.

On the historical date that Herr Stein finally made his mad dash for freedom, he drank strong Western coffee for breakfast and packed a last valuable manuscript in his briefcase. He was not the slightest bit nervous or sentimental at leaving forever. He put on his most photogenic black suit, which was a bit fine for a library visit, so he pulled a crumpled raincoat on over it. He ignored his mother's protest about the coat. During the twenty-minute journey from East to West, he ignored her altogether. The border guards were indifferent.

On reaching the Western side of the wall, Herr Stein was suddenly in too much of a hurry to drop his mother off exactly at her destination. Instead he let her out in front of Woolworth's, two blocks from her friend's house. He might as well have locked her behind bars for the next two hours; he knew Woolworth's would hold her until he had the scenario set up. He drove on to an acquaintance who worked at home and had a photogenic living room. This was a psychologist. Herr Stein interrupted the doctor during therapy. "I'm awfully sorry, Dr. Rumina," he said. "Can I just use your phone?"

Dr. Rumina made his patients wait. Herr Stein called his mother's girlfriend and established to his satisfaction that Frau Stein had not arrived there yet. "When she reaches you, tell her to come to see me at Dr. Rumina's," he said and spelled the address out. He refused to give the telephone number. "She shouldn't call me because I have to keep the line here free. She should just come. She'll be surprised at some news I have." He checked his watch. "There's plenty of time for her to take the bus here."

His next call was to the tabloids. More patients came and had to wait. The press arrived. By the time his mother rang the doorbell, just once, with that characteristic modesty Herr Stein recognized and hated, everything was set up. He signaled the photographers that Frau Stein was at the door. When she walked in he kissed her, as he had been instructed. The bulbs flashed. Someone pressed a bouquet of flowers into her arms. The bulbs flashed again, in ecstasy. "Mama, I'm free!" Herr Stein cried, his forehead wet, his eyes dry, although he would have preferred it the other way around. "It's like a fairy tale come true!" he added. The journalists noted this for their headlines.

"But," Frau Stein whispered, "I don't know what my boy is talking about."

Dr. Rumina's patients were visible in the background, perched on sofa arms or leaning against the grand piano, holding glasses of champagne, mental health glowing at all the excitement.

But Herr Stein dismissed them when he had to use the phone. Calls number three, four, and five went to friends keeping his possessions. Suddenly he knew every item he had "forgotten," down to the cuff links. His mother was audible in the kitchen. "Why didn't he tell me? I could have brought him his warm things, at least."

"I have my warm things!" he called.

"You must discuss your feelings openly with your son," Dr. Rumina counseled.

"Pull yourself together," Herr Stein remarked, putting the phone down and coming into the kitchen. "I had to do it this way. You would never have managed to cross the border if you had known. You would have bawled the whole story to the first border guard. Can you make me a cup of coffee? As a senior citizen, you can come and visit me as often as you like." He withdrew hastily when he saw the tears permanent and stagnant on her cheeks. He had expected her to be grateful to learn the news personally from him, not from the radio the next morning. She was quite a killjoy. He headed for the phone.

Call number seven went to his tax adviser. Herr Stein was about to make a plane reservation to fly to Frankfurt that evening when his mother marched out of the kitchen, calm restored, and said, "Make it for tomorrow, dear. Poor thing, you need a rest. Think of your heart. I'll stay with you till tomorrow, make sure you have some peace and quiet tonight. No one will make any trouble for me at the border tomorrow. I'll tell them I was sick with a cold." It wouldn't be hard to persuade them, her eyes were so red from crying.

Herr Stein postponed his flight until the next day, dispatching Dr. Rumina with his mother to buy her a change of clothes and a nightgown, since she insisted on staying on with him. He realized the pretty old woman elicited people's sympathy. Call number eight went to the West Berlin authorities, telling them that he was defecting. The officer had already heard the news on the radio and said, "Welcome, Herr Stein, with open arms. To a fairy tale come true."

As an East German, Herr Stein was regarded by the West German government as a citizen of the Bundesrepublik. He could have his West German passport at once. First a little interview with the officials, nothing serious, it could be done in Frankfurt. Herr Stein was sure he knew all the right answers. With his host out of the house, he relaxed.

Soon a young woman arrived to clean the windows. With minimum concentration, Herr Stein made crude advances to her while she was standing on the ladder. She locked herself in the bathroom, terrified by the long, thin man with the strange accent. Never mind. Herr Stein was reveling in his freedom.

The day passed quickly. In the late evening, mother and son settled down into twin collapsible cots which their host had set up for them in the living room. Dr. Rumina did not really like overnight guests because of the inconvenience with the bathrooms, and irritation was starting to outweigh pleasure at having front-row seats to a real defection. Herr Stein, for his part, would have preferred a plusher bed for his first night as a free man. He could barely fit his long frame onto the mattress and it squeaked when he moved. His mother's bed instantly answered in a communication he did not wish. "You must go to sleep now, you poor boy, such a big day tomorrow," she repeated. He stopped worrying about her return to East Berlin. He didn't care if they reduced her to tears and panic with questions and lamps—she deserved harassment.

He awoke in the morning tied up in his sheets, his mother's

thumbs massaging his temples. She murmured, "I'm defecting too. I'm not leaving you here all alone, like a motherless child, in this strange country."

"You can't possibly defect!" he said, instantly alert. "As an old lady you are *allowed* to go back over the border anytime, back and forth, back and forth. You are even allowed to move west with all your worldly goods—except the silver fox. They'll be delighted to help you move because it saves them from paying you a pension, and your apartment is vacated for some official who's been waiting. That is why you shouldn't move. You'll have problems here. Insurance! You have to pay for insurance. If they pay you a pension here, it won't get you far. You'll be impoverished."

But she had already contacted the press:

MOM JOINS SON IN DEFECTION

MATHEMATICIAN'S MOTHER DEFECTS WITHOUT A SUITCASE

"We can share an apartment here too," she said, a stoic, remembering that the baby's birth had been worse. "I don't need a coat. I care about you and making sure you have a warm meal to come to anytime you want."

MOM GIVES UP FUR!

Herr Stein was too weak to object. It proved no consolation when the maid returned and moped, hoping he would make another pass at her. She had seen his face in the morning's tabloids and was wildly flattered by Herr Stein's advances of the previous day. But he no longer noticed her. His ebullience was gone.

The government was in cahoots with his mother. They gave senior citizens a comparable pension at once on reaching the West. There was a lot of red tape to get through, but not enough to kill an old woman. Herr Stein breezed through several interviews, in which he managed to prove he had only political and financial motives for defecting. No one ever suspected Herr Stein's real reason. Everyone was very helpful. A city senator offered Herr Stein an apartment in one of his own privately owned buildings. Three rooms, newly renovated, at a reasonable rent, given the central address, where the wealthier residents lived. The housing market was tough in West Berlin. The senator was an important man with connections in academic circles, so Herr Stein had no alternative but to accept his offer. His mother needed several months to pack the place with heavy furniture and carpeting.

Of course, his powers of benign neglect did not diminish. He kept his apartment in Frankfurt secret, and he kept his relationships to various women vague. Only the faceless names he occasionally called at the press knew where he was. He no longer gave personal interviews because he found that reporters—somber, critical agents of power—didn't write as favorably about him after they had seen him.

His mother was melancholic. She took little pleasure in all her new things because she missed the old ones. Their elevator always functioned, but they lived on the first floor and never used it. Sometimes the tears were so thick in her eyes that she could not find her way outside to shop. No one made note of this. In the West they seldom had visitors, and the Sony radio did not have to be turned up for private conversations. Now she exercised her paranoia worrying about price hikes and missed bargains. It was some consolation to her that she could keep track of her boy's whereabouts by reading the newspaper.

After two years, though, the newspaper stopped keeping track of Herr Stein. Herr Stein worried about his taxes; secreting money from the tax authorities proved too hard, because they were always snuffling for information and latched onto the smallest infraction. The refugees would never have been so ungrateful as to complain, however. Herr and Frau Stein were forced to live happily ever after.

The

Passion of

Nanny Jackie

Nanny Jackie was the latest in a long line of professionals who looked after the poet when no one else would. The poet's ex-wife hired her on the basis of a photograph of a beaming round face. The British nanny agency that sent the photo described Nanny Jackie as twenty-five years old, in "the British tradition of service," honest, Catholic, reliable, slim, "a happy girl." It neglected to say she came from a home in Belfast where "broken" applied to the arms and noses of the family beaten by a brawling father.

The agency had not asked Nanny Jackie whether she would enjoy working for a man. She would not, although she fancied a church wedding someday. The agency had not inquired whether Nanny Jackie liked mankind in general. She did not. She placed most people on the negative side of what life had to offer. Also on the negative side were her wispy brown hair, her inability to tan evenly, the fact that "slim" applied only to the top third of her, and that she had never had a boyfriend. On the positive side, she did not want a boyfriend, and her talents—cheerfulness and industriousness—were qualities rewarded by a steady income. Also positive was that while an employer readily developed a dependency on a nanny, a nanny remained without ties.

Before joining the poet in New York, Nanny Jackie had demonstrated her independence to her satisfaction with single working mothers in northern England. She had liked reaching a mutual climax of bad feelings with them and then leaving at the moment when it caused maximum discomfort. Nanny Jackie's professional cheerfulness was, in truth, not entirely under her control. Regularly, once a month, it left her. She became grumpy. Since she remained otherwise devoid of strong emotions, she was extremely conscious of her bad moods and gave them free rein. A past employer had put the matter succinctly: "She suffers a premenstrual tension that could knock the Russian forces out of Afghanistan."

The agency had discretely omitted this reference from her file. Fair's fair, they had not told Nanny Jackie much about the job, either, other than that it was unusual, looking after an ancient and famous poet in New York City. They did not warn her that the poet would not take an interest in her beyond her physical presence, not even enough to produce mutual bad feelings. The poet was too preoccupied with himself. He had reached ninety-two when Nanny Jackie entered his life, and his inabilities (he had no disabilities yet) made him frantic and sleepy by turn. When frantic, he dragged himself by cane through the five-room apartment a divorce had left to him, railing against death's dominion. Nanny Jackie signed a one-year contract she did not consider binding, settled in, and began at once to list the pros and cons about the job in her head, which was her only way of establishing whether she liked her employer and her situation.

She placed the chafing of an old man in the plus column because she found it rather amusing. It was easy enough to wrest control of him when he was too agitated by intercepting his pacing with an open box of chocolates, an old trick she had learned with preschoolers. Chocolate became her weapon, it calmed the poet, the gooier the better. He removed his teeth for full appreciation. She could tell he was entirely calmed down when he left the chocolate box unguarded. Then she helped herself. She loved chocolate too, another item in the plus column being that she could buy the best Swiss chocolate out of her shopping allowance and no one objected; buying children candy often incurred an employer's wrath.

Nevertheless, the negative column quickly grew longer than the positive one. The poet had no visitors except for his young, coolly observant ex-wife, so that meant Nanny Jackie's social life was miserable. On her day off, she could take the subway down to Macy's and buy postcards to buck up her spirits. The work schedule left plenty of time to write these cards but it was otherwise tedious and repetitious—helping a cranky old man get washed, watching him shave himself to shreds, applying plasters to his face, searching for his teeth on hands and knees, talking him out of wearing his best black suit in favor of a easier-to-clean tweed, turning the television on and off when he shouted, executing "the usual household duties," which included dusting his volumes of poetry while he watched and criticized, taking a cane walker out for a walk once a day, showing him his bills, watching him curse his bills, helping a fuming old man pay his bills, and, finally, trying to quiet him down when night came and fear of death waited in his pillow.

Night provided the worst moments of the job. From the very first evening he had one thing in his head: She should sit on his bed or, even better, in his bed. He said it as an order, grim as a brigadier, that it was her job to sit there next to him and hold his hand. Otherwise he couldn't sleep, and he had to have his sleep, or he couldn't think the next day. She pretended not to understand his New England accent, fluffed the pillow for him, and murmured reassurance. She could sleep soundly, knowing he was unable to stand up without his cane, and she would take the precaution of hiding it for the night.

On the plus side was the salary, huge by British standards, as well as the fact that she had her own room in a pleasant apartment and what agencies call "free travel," a round-trip ticket to New York paid for by the poet's family. New York was a plus, the way Manchester had been, because it was not Belfast and because it was her sister Moira's unfulfilled dream to see Macy's.

On the minus side, nannying was not walking the street as a police woman, which had been her ambition since the New Year's Eve that she as a small child could not intervene when British soldiers thrashed her father unconscious for making obscene gestures at them with a broom. As always, Nanny Jackie had this column of her feelings itemized within her first months of work. Looming large and final in the minus column was that she hated the poet and felt married to him.

II.

It took only a few months for the poet to decline to a point where his ex-wife no longer felt it necessary to visit him at all.

He could only walk with two canes, holding one in each hand; he needed hours of help with the toilet; and his eyes, glazed by dependency, followed Nanny Jackie's movements. His ears, as well as they were able, stayed tuned to the sound of her. When she went out on errands without him, she moved a chair to the door where he could sit, waiting for her to come back. If this was a kindness on her part, she attributed it to her good mood of the moment and month and felt he was putting a strain on that commodity. When being tactful he called her "dear" or "my darling" because he could not remember her name. Untactful, he called her Else, the name of his ex-wife, or Myra, the name of his deceased sister. The list she kept in her head of the pros and cons of the job had grown longer on the con side. Walking with two canes. Almost blind. Almost deaf. Instead of railing against death, he called her wrong names. The ceaseless, restless nights when he called her and begged her to sit on the edge of his bed, and then under the covers with him. Not even the hope of a visitor.

Periodically she lost her good mood. New York was as dull as Belfast, the poet no more deserving than her father. She sat in front of the television puffed up like a sick pigeon and too lethargic even to switch channels. Her face became bloated, her hair hung in limp wads around her shoulders. Then the rage set in, and she told the poet that she was out of sorts. He did not react at all. So she hated him for not taking her seriously, the con side tipped heavily, and she decided to quit. But not just yet. "Our Jackie's going to make something of herself," her father had always bragged to her mother and her elder sister. "Keep your eyes on her, our Moira, she's going to outshine you. I know she has a future." And when she accepted the job in America, he got drunk to celebrate and tottered through the streets, yelling, "Our Jackie's made it!" So Nanny Jackie couldn't quit straight away.

She tried to find a way for the poet to share her misery: she told him she was leaving him to work in a police precinct. He became hysterical. She brought out the chocolates. Then she refused to take him for his daily walk because, she said, the street smelled so dreadful that it would make her sick. He did not apologize for the smell of the street, but he did not object to staying indoors either. For three days she was unpleasant, then on the fourth day she was exhausted but sweet tempered, relieved to be getting something over with. After that she was herself again: cheerful, robust, rejecting, and tolerating her grim but financially rewarding present.

So they lived for a period of about six months.

Without once touching him more than duty required, she became intimate with him: she knew his weight, and his smell and the noises he made. She knew the texture of his hair, of his face, of his long nose, of his thin lower arms. She knew how his legs, in their baggy trousers, dangled when the chair was too high. She knew his mouth, loose and toothless. She knew the look in his eyes when he watched television and boredom nudged him over into sleep.

Occasionally she mobilized her thoughts to ask herself why, given all the cons, she did not extremely mind her situation. Then she recalled walking into the living room in Belfast and seeing her sister and father in an odd, stiff embrace. Her father had his back turned to Jackie as he bent in front of his eldest daughter and kissed her child's chest. Nanny Jackie remembered our Moira's face, as seen above his busy bald head. Affection was confusing. Now our Moira was married with four sons. Surrounded by men, she would never see Macy's.

III.

Just when Macy's was beginning to bore Nanny Jackie, a blow to the plus column, the poet actually had a visitor. It had been a normal day, of a normal week, of a normal month. Nanny Jackie was slimming. The food she ate was part of the salary and during her first few months in New York Nanny Jackie had paid herself overtime. But the need to plunder her employer had decreased lately, and she had dieted, the way her mother did: something cyclical, like drought on the bog, noticed as it was already ending, soon forgotten.

The day of the visit she was executing the whipped-potato-and-applesauce scheme, which suited the poet's needs as well. She watched him eat, dabbing at his chin when required. He ate listlessly, without interest, and he wouldn't take one bite if she wasn't sitting next to him, urging him on. Afterward she helped him to his bed. He lowered his backside as a great weight and she heaved his legs up for him. He lay there with his eyes closed, groaning. Ghastly. Every day, this; he called it a rest. He claimed he needed it to clear his mind. As if—she thought, and so on.

He was lying there while she leafed through a magazine when the doorbell rang. On the other side of the peephole stood someone with long black hair and a red coat who introduced herself as Miss Paul, a friend of the poet's ex-wife. She proved to be a vivacious, pretty woman not much older than Nanny Jackie, and from the first instant it was obvious that she respected the poet. She apologized for disturbing, claimed she was just passing by, strictly an impulse visit. She dangled a boxed cake. Nanny Jackie knew no one just dropped in on an invalid.

The visitor apparently knew who Nanny Jackie was and so did not trouble to ask her name. She stepped over the threshold.

How is he? I haven't seen him in awhile. She rushed past Nanny Jackie, steering correctly into the poet's room. Sounds of confused appreciation from the poet. Nanny Jackie on Miss Paul's trail.

Now there was some further sound of conversation. Nanny Jackie was not used to it. Questions reached her ears: Wouldn't we like to have some coffee and cake? Suggestions circulated: Come on, sit up, that's right, lean on me if you like.

Miss Paul led the poet to the dining room, helped him into the Harvard chair Nanny Jackie had found much too low for him, and then this guest bustled into the kitchen and put the kettle on. Nanny Jackie hastily set three places at the table, Miss Paul beamed at her, and they sat down.

The conversation was animated. Miss Paul knew all the poet's books and she slogged through his muddy attention span asking him about his past and his present, even daring to inquire what he was working on now; well, if he wasn't working, then what was he thinking?

The poet kept feeding her preposterous curiosity with replies. It seems he had been thinking about the unlikeliest things: nature, time, civilization. About nothing so simple as the neighborhood, which was Miss Paul's latest topic: it had changed, hadn't it? Mindful of his bad hearing, she called out all her questions, her eyes and red lipstick sparkling. But then he stopped talking, he looked around vaguely and said, "Lately I've been thinking about the Other Side. And about my mother and father and brother, who are waiting for me there."

Tears banged into Miss Paul's eyes. She swallowed her tea briskly. She did not ask him another question.

But she did not need to. The poet prattled on and on about his poems, the influence of his mother, of Wordsworth, of the symbolists. He was slurping his coffee and gobbling his cake. You should really write another poem, she said, about being old. One more, he agreed, before I cannot.

Suddenly he stood up from the table. Nanny Jackie rushed to fetch his two canes, but it was too late for canes, the poet was lumbering around the room on his own. Abruptly he stopped, turned his large white head back to gaudy Miss Paul, and said, "Old age is not gay!"

Miss Paul did not move, and Nanny Jackie grabbed her chance, springing to the poet's side and helping him to his bed. He would need a long rest now, after this stress. She was strangely aware of her own palm on his arm. Somehow, somewhere in herself, like a silent nudging she felt her fondness for his thin white arms and frail body, and for his profile that she knew in its agony. She pooh-poohed his fame. Then she directed to Miss Paul a lynching look.

IV.

In his last month of life, the poet enjoyed himself. Nanny Jackie doted on him, without knowing why. His limbs had a softness and floppiness now that he could no longer move them himself. Hair grew anarchistically out of his nose and ears, there was something rather awesome about it and she did not try to interfere. She took care of him, washed him, and put his best black jacket on him. No use saving it.

Time passed slowly now. She forgot to take days off; she either suppressed or did not notice her monthly humors. They hardly spoke to each other anymore; Nanny Jackie watched him closely and knew exactly when he wanted something before he needed to ask for it. But no, she would not lie down with him, as he still asked, when the fear of death raked him and he reached for her hand. She let him hold her hand. Sometimes she reached for his.

One evening Nanny Jackie was reading a magazine, sitting in a chair next to the poet's bed. Suddenly his chest heaved several times, and thereafter he was dead.

Now, finally, she did as he had begged so often, she sat down on the bed with him, and then, after a moment, she settled under the covers next to him. He was warm, pleasingly so, a perfect temperature, and his skin was soft, and his hair smelled of something pleasant, his own smell. So she put her arms around him and laid her head on his shoulder, and she lay with him that way all night.

My Most Memorable Character

At first the words had just passed through Freddy's thoughts like bubbles through seltzer:

. . . So Freddy, let's get cracking: make the bed OK? OK boy? Yes yes, here we go, my goodness my dear boy, today you are looking good, what'll Dorothy say? Freddy, you look so nice! With that dumb smile. The milk's turned. Again. You must get a fan, yes I really must go, oh golly, golly, nice purple sky today, have a look, looks like the priest's robes, like God's bottom, God is sitting on the world today as though it were his pot, so we are, oh please, Freddy, don't blaspheme, this heat! Must get a new fan because the milk turns, a fortune in milk. . . .

That was when his sister Dorothy still visited him every day. She came over during her lunch break from the hospital, walking fast down Haven Avenue, carrying a neat paper bag with his sandwich. As a rule he didn't like to eat, so he was fastidious about what he did eat. The sandwich always had to be bologna and on-white-with-lettuce. His sister had learned. He ate it while she was there so they wouldn't have to talk very much. He let her prattle. He let her sit in his leather television chair with the seven tiny rips on the right arm while he took the plastic kitchen chair which was neither gray nor green. He was always glad to see her but he preferred the dialogue in his head to hers. He ate as slowly as possible because no one could expect him to speak when his mouth was full. When she left he was glad, and then he missed her, wondering, What's she doing right now, right this instant? And he pictured her at the doctor's office, typing away or pushing through her own front door, turning on the television just at the same time he was, laughing at jokes he felt were not funny but she would like. He never laughed aloud anymore but always in his head: ha ha ha.

Nor did he cry when Dorothy died. He understood that she had been very unhappy. Everyone in their family was unhappy and one person's unhappiness breeds another's. He found everyone's unhappiness uninteresting, including his own. He made the bologna sandwiches himself from then on, buying the ingredients from Lunger's Grocery at the corner. Lunger was doddering, his head weaved, he spoke neither English nor German correctly anymore and therefore spoke as little as possible. Freddy knew how Dorothy had shopped there, so he did the same, imitating her sandwiches exactly, striving even for the ridiculous wilt of lettuce on top. When he ate the sandwich immediately after making it, he found the lettuce was too crisp against his teeth. He concluded that he had to prepare it over breakfast, just as his sister must have done:

Be sure to smear just the right amount. Oh Freddy! You've made a mistake again: push the bowl aside, now you've spilled your Coke, I *am* clumsy sometimes.

He pulled the shades down, blocking the sun and the black tar of Haven Avenue, its facades of rusty fire escapes and laundry, its disheveled cars, and then, with caution, he buttered the bread. This was not quick work. He knew Dorothy had always taken time and care making his lunch every day. He ate the sandwich when the clock said twelve thirty, after pulling the shade up again because the sun had moved to the western side of Haven Avenue.

There come mornings in the American city which are not unlike the mornings in Cairo or Bombay: You have a sense of living in the street. Sleeping by the open window, the smells of the city awaken you as the gutter warms up. Later, trucks mill by your head, babies scream at you through the window, intimate voices address you. And soon, if you have still not gotten out of bed, the heat comes through like a hand.

On mornings like these the thoughts running through Freddy's head often discussed the problem of buying a fan. Freddy knew he would have to speak to the salesman. He could figure out which model he wanted from the television commercials, he could know exactly how much he'd have to spend from the money he received once a month. But suppose something went wrong, suppose they tried to talk him out of what he wanted, or laughed at him for his choice or for his accent. Dorothy really ought to have done this for him, she loved to talk and loved to shop. Now it was June and July and the milk turned sour after a few hours. It had been too much trouble to ask her, and then. Twice a day Freddy went to buy milk and Coke, bologna and lettuce from the silent Lunger. After returning, he al-

ways rested for a while in his television chair, sitting there in his
undershorts and slippers. He was careful about wearing slippers
because of the germs on the floor. By the time he had recovered,
the milk was already at room temperature and when he poured
the Coke into his glass the dark liquid bubbled volcanically.

It had occurred to Freddy several months into the summer
that he had not spoken to anyone for several weeks. This pleased
him all through July. Then he wondered how long he could go
without having to open his mouth to speak at all, he wondered
about this for several days . . . Oh loathsome, the way people
always want to talk . . .

He kept track and succeeded for another month. He was
watching television all the time now, not even turning it off
during the hours there were no programs. He found the crack-
ling of his television so suspenseful and one could have such a
great surprise when the voices suddenly began to talk again,
. . . like mother coming home . . . that he often lay awake
nights listening to it.

The voice in his thoughts had in-depth conversations with
Captain Kangaroo in the morning, with the quiz masters of afternoon, with the comedy characters of the evening. And then one
day the voice said: For two months you haven't said a word, can
you still? And Freddy suddenly worried.

That day he said something to himself, just to see. He said:
"Eee." It came out at a very high pitch and sounded mostly like
a squeak. But it satisfied him. His voice worked. He squeaked
again. After that, whenever he did not hear his voice for several
minutes, he squeaked and felt reassured: he was still all there.
Meanwhile, it no longer really seemed necessary to eat his lunch
at the kitchen table. So he left the shade down at twelve thirty

and ate his sandwich on the leather television chair. There were never any crumbs to sweep away afterward, so he returned the plate with its white giraffes to the table and used it again at his next meal. The only hardship of life came when he went out. Since his voice had fallen into disuse, he feared meeting his neighbors more than ever. He avoided them with calculation.

Suppose she's there, sitting by the big washer. I bet she's gone to the garbage, not a good time for me to . . .

The neighbors said it smells funny in there, sometimes he squeaks! But they were not curious and avoided him when he went to empty the garbage.

It was just short of the Jewish New Year. The words were still bubbling through Freddy's thoughts. One morning he was seated, his chest bared against the heat, watching the *Captain Kangaroo Show*. The captain was telling one of his puppets a great joke. He was warming up to the punch line and the three-minute break, saying, "Now, boys and girls," sweating with restrained laughter. Then suddenly his voice disappeared. While his lips continued to form vowels and syllables, the captain was mute. The apartment was quiet. Freddy started up. He jumped out of his chair so frantically that next door they heard the rumble of furniture and wondered. He rammed the TV volume on high. But the captain, now holding his sides with laughter, was utterly silent. The room felt dead weight with silence. Now Freddy felt the pressure of his voice. The words were rushing like bubbles through seltzer. "Eeee," he said. Nothing. The words were rushing.

. . . How can it first the fan the salesman on 181st Street

with its sign the store is huge the salesman will have a beard and, "No thank you, I don't want this model I want that one," I should never go out I must never go out I must never never go that damned Dorothy I'll blaspheme if I want to . . .

The dialogue in Freddy's head was bubbling out through his mouth. And Freddy heard it and panicked, scampering out to the street without closing the door. But when he entered the heat, he forgot his fear, for he heard the voice and it was after all a most familiar voice, he marveled as it appealed to the wall, to the sidewalk, and to all the familiar strangers the injustice that Dorothy had died, the fan had broken down, and now the captain had stopped his joke just short of the punch line.

Freddy's thoughts running uncontrolled through his mouth prompted twelve calls—seven to the superintendent, four to the police and one to the fire department. He was taken somewhere. The superintendent cleaned up the little flat after him. He sent the welfare people a bill for three days' work. He kept the television and the fan, fixed them, and sold them two weeks later. The kitchen table was taken by Mrs. Meyerhof from 122, the chair by Mr. Gonzales of 11, who used it as a stepladder. No one wanted Freddy's leather chair. Beneath the cushion were several inches of crumbs that no one had the stomach to clean away.

The

Smuggled

Wedding

Ring

A story in two parts, with two chocolate bars; two kinds of cotton wool; two families, one Russian-Jewish, one German; two gold rings, one fake, one real; and a lot of ambition and disillusionment.

1.

A Russian-Jewish family has just moved into a sixty-square-meter apartment in West Berlin. The building is brand new—that means it's small, economical, and smells of concrete. It is the classical *Neubau*. The term produces a wrinkle of disgust on the well-nourished face of any fashionable Berliner. This kind of native would never live in a building dating after the First World War, when the taste for parquet and individual stucco on high ceilings was defeated by economic necessity. But to Micha Zinochky and his wife and daughter, *"neu"* is a word with aura.

The Zinochkys adore the number of their rooms, three; they respect the smooth gray linoleum, attend the roar of the windowless bathroom's ventilator, and watch for the transformation of the electric stove rings from gray to orange.

The family has few possessions, and what it has comes in threes: three plates, three cups, three pots, and so on. The Soviet Union allowed each member of the family to take one suitcase of clothing, two books, and a total of five grams of precious metal out of the country. The family left an extensive library in the Ukraine last year as well as their daughter's toys, their friends and relations, and almost all their valuables. This was the cost, they knew it beforehand, and they accepted the bill. Their relatives could follow them, and as far as material goods were concerned, they expected to get their money back in the West. The only items they really missed were their wedding rings.

Micha Zinochky discovered the necessity for a wedding ring relatively late, just before his twenty-fifth birthday, during a routine inspection of his favorite reflection: Micha after a bath. The stocky, swarthy medical doctor with the small eyes realized that his black curls had changed. They were beginning to thin. His curls had been his trademark since his childhood. When he was in trouble, his curls recalled his mother to her senses. Often his relatives had gathered, so it seemed to him, only to stand him in their midst and admire the tightly curled black silk on his head. The night before he saw that his curls were mortal, he had taken out a nurse in the Sambor hospital where he worked.

Her name was Marya, she was a tiny, delicate person with large brown eyes and chestnut hair teased in the beehive style popular in Sambor in the seventies. Micha scarcely noticed her charms, he had only invited her out to show up another nurse who had recently refused him. He had spent a pleasant evening preoccupied with the impression he was making, never dreaming of the shock that awaited him on the other side of the night. Marya had noticed his absentmindedness but not interpreted it; she was just eighteen.

The next afternoon, after a heavy lunch in the hospital mess hall, he stopped off at Marya's ward and proposed to her as she emptied a bedpan. She giggled and said yes, but not right now. She meant it just like that, a naive creature who accepted without complaining when others made decisions for her. Her "yes" did not assuage his uneasiness. He wanted to prove his status, married man, in a big way. He bought the heaviest wedding rings in all Kiev. They weighed ten grams each, with notches in the side, and had a broad, flat, polished expanse in which he could see his reflection.

For a while, Micha's uneasiness disappeared. He was sure of himself again. He had thinning hair, but he had changed his life to suit the new circumstance, he had become a husband. Then one day he noticed how deep a certain furrow in his forehead had become; he had been monitoring this since it made its appearance during his late teens, a faint line, a threat never made good until suddenly, so it seemed, when it turned into a deep wrinkle. His uneasiness returned. He had to change his life.

So they had a baby, a girl with black curls, and his restlessness was cured for a while. He put on weight, which proved his role, doting father. But then the restlessness returned. Marya had developed the figure of a woman who carries heavy loads: she was wide and square, her hands rough. Her hair was too dry to wear in a bouffant, and the skin under her chin sagged. "It comes from waiting on line and worrying so much," she apologized to her husband. He didn't mind her appearance as much as he minded his own. He was just thirty when he began finding white hairs at his temples. Every morning he spent extra minutes at the mirror pulling them out, his hands sweaty with worry and disgust.

He was employed as a medical specialist, one of the lower-paid professions in the Soviet Union, where 75 to 80 percent of all doctors were women. His field was male venereal diseases, his salary 120 rubles a month, the price of a pair of expensive women's boots. Dr. Zinochky had learned to supplement his income. He knew that some diseases, requiring registration, embarrassed his patients and annoyed their spouses. For a small gratuity he renamed a diagnosis; for a larger one he treated a patient privately at his home. His excellent reputation reached all the way to Kiev.

Some patients paid in other currency. One sufferer was a housing official; he found the doctor a very desirable apartment in Sambor opposite a row of stores. From the kitchen window Marya could see what the trucks were delivering. The Zinochkys were the first in town, next to those who had bribed the sales clerk, to know when there was meat or fresh fruit. Once they spotted a shipment of raisins long before anyone else did. They felt forced by principle—raisins were rare—to buy the entire shipment. They ate raisins for weeks. After that the word *raisin* made them gag.

For New Year's Eve, 1986, Micha was not able to buy any champagne. That night his sobriety was killing him. Another year wasted. He decided the time had come to make a move so big that he would not notice the pain of his fortieth birthday. A few weeks after New Year's, Micha applied to emigrate to Israel.

His decision was newsworthy in Sambor: some considered it scandal, others a political item. "I thought you were Ukrainian," a cook at the mess hall remarked as she was loading his plate with potatoes. "Being Jewish isn't a nationality," she said, "it's an exit visa." He stopped eating at the mess hall and brought bread from home. At school his daughter's classmates warned her that she would be drafted into the Israeli army and probably killed in Lebanon. Only Marya was strangely indifferent to what people thought of them. At night she listened to Micha's stories of woe and seemed completely unaffected. She slept like a top. Once she told him a joke that she'd apparently known for years and never bothered to recite:

Moishe applies to emigrate, and the KGB interviews him. "Moishe," they say, "you have a good job, a nice flat, enough to eat, why do you want to leave?"

Moishe says, "I can't remember." But he refuses to withdraw his application.

So the KGB invites him in again. "Moishe, such a nice flat you have, and your own car, Moishe, why do you want to leave?"

And Moishe can't remember. But he refuses to withdraw his application. A third time the KGB invites Moishe in for a chat.

"Moishe, why, why do you want to leave, when you have it so good here?"

"Yes," answers Moishe, "I have it good here. I can't for the life of me remember why I wanted to leave."

"Damn Jews," says the KGB man, "spoiled rotten."

"Ah," says Moishe, "I just remembered why I wanted to go."

Micha laughed at the punch line and then he was furious at her. "You tell jokes so flatly you don't deserve to know any," he said. He did not realize that his wife was Jewish until many years

of marriage had passed. Her parents had died during her childhood and she had only her father's sister and a brother, who had
never discussed such things. According to her passport she was
Ukrainian too. But she had picked up a lot of Yiddish from her
aunt. It had been her suggestion on New Year's Eve that if they
were allowed to go to Israel then they should try to end up in
Germany. Someone had told her that the Jewish community in
Berlin was very helpful. She had bits of information in her head
like that, Micha didn't know how they'd gotten in there.

They toasted the new year with vodka, and Micha said,
"Swear you won't mention this to my parents! You know what
my father will call me? A traitor."

His parents lived in a village outside of Sambor where he
had grown up. It seemed to Micha proof of the correctness of his
decision that the news of it never reached his parents' ears.
Aside from tolerable teasing, the family experienced no reper-
cussions at all, nor did they receive an answer from the emigra-
tion office.

About six months after putting in his application to emigrate,
Dr. Zinochky was summoned from the hospital to attend to vic-
tims of a "factory accident." The police came for him. The drive
proved to be rather long; he was taken to Chernobyl. This was
about three months after the nuclear accident there and venereal disease was rampant among the clean-up crew, who had
nothing to do during the evenings in the deserted city. Dr. Zinochky stayed there a month. He did not wear protective clothing and he was not informed about radiation hazards. Shortly
after Micha returned to his hometown, the Zinochkys received
notice that their exit visas were ready and they had two weeks to
pack.

It was a sticky summer evening when Micha Zinochky put on his best jacket and went to see his parents in the two-room village house where he had grown up. His father was gardening, his mother making cherry jam. His father knew something was wrong as soon as he saw Micha's face. He borrowed his son's sleeve to wipe the sweat from his face and led him indoors. While Micha Zinochky recited all the reasons for emigrating west, his father smiled bitterly. Micha's jacket hung over a chair; his father picked it up, fingered the poor material, and then bunched it to his eyes. He wouldn't say a word.

"He thinks you're a traitor," his mother said. She had forgiven him his decision instantly. She announced that they would follow Micha to Germany as soon as they could.

Two weeks later Micha, Marya, and their eight-year-old daughter left the Soviet Union. The wedding rings that had proven such a consolation to Micha were many grams over the limit, so Micha had Marya's ring melted down into two five-gram rings and they each wore one half. At the last minute Marya decided to take instead the gold earrings Micha had given her after they announced their engagement, and to leave the diminished wedding ring with a friend.

When they reached the border to Hungary, Soviet officials weighed the earrings and found them to be a few milligrams over the permitted five grams. They took the earrings, cut off the bottoms, and allowed Marya to keep what remained.

Micha Zinochky is the only child of Ivan Zinochky, of whom it is often said in the family, "He's crazy." In particular Ivan's wife, Micha's mother, Helena, likes to complain that her husband is mad. The complaints began after Micha left the Soviet Union and Helena wanted to follow him to the West. After all, she argued, one son, one life. We have to stay together. But Ivan wouldn't hear of leaving his dacha and fruit garden near Sambor. Especially not to go to Germany. He had fought against the Germans during World War II. A German soldier had shot him in the back at Stalingrad. He had been dragged off the field and had enjoyed the fruits of this injury ever after—he had a special pension, took all forms of public transportation (including planes) for free, and received extra portions of meat weekly. When he wore the emblem of a wounded veteran on his jacket, he could go to the head of every queue. Why should he leave?

"Your father has gone stark-raving mad," Helena wrote to her son.

"Dear Father, you must pull yourself together, and take a chance, and come to Berlin," wrote Micha Zinochky to his father, who celebrated his seventy-fifth birthday under siege from his family.

The conflict was waged carefully in the mail, which one presumed a public medium. "You will never find a job in the West," wrote Ivan. "And we are old people and will starve to death."

"I am already working," fired back Micha Zinochky, "and so is Marya, she is a nurse. We are saving money to support you."

This was a partial lie. Only Marya is working, but not as a nurse. True is that they have raised their standard of living. The family receives welfare funds that equal more than twice as much as they earned working full time in the Soviet Union. In addition, the Jewish community gives them money for Pesach and Hanukkah and has helped Marya find work; she is employed as a maid by several families. She is so eager and thorough, in fact, that she commands top salaries.

True is that they are saving money. Marya passes on every penny to her husband, who places it in a shoe box for safekeeping. He is saving up to buy himself a car and then to pay for his German lessons. Micha will have the most expensive German lessons in town because he cannot not qualify to work as a doctor until his German is fluent. It doesn't matter about Marya's German.

While Marya goes off to work for him and their daughter makes rapid progress at school, he watches television. If Marya doesn't return punctually, he calls her employers, trying to find her. Often she is strolling along the Ku'damm, Berlin's main shopping street, window shopping.

She has never bought anything for herself, however, not even something small. In the West she can't afford to buy anything on impulse. In the East she shopped constantly; in the West husband and wife discuss every purchase for weeks before making it. It took them months to find the bed they wanted.

The purchase of a mahogany bedroom suite was their entrance to the consumer world. The double bed had a built-in radio, lighting, and a mirror in the headboard. The matching wardrobe had six gleaming doors on silent hinges. The suite cost them their entire welfare furniture allowance.

The price included delivery. After the delivery boys had come and gone, the Zinochkys saw their mistake: the room was too small to contain both the bed and the wardrobe. They fit only when the wardrobe stood opposite the bed. This did not leave enough space to open the middle four doors. But they had only enough clothes to fill two sections of the wardrobe anyway.

The Zinochkys let their daughter sleep in the bed and made themselves a bed of blankets in the living room. They began to plot the acquisition of a second bed.

"The old fool!" Micha Zinochky called his father when he read Ivan Zinochky's decision not to leave the Soviet Union. "He has no idea what it's like here. About the toilet paper, and the new apartment building, not about anything!"

"What he's really afraid of is the immigration, Ivan. You should never have told him about the wedding rings," Marya replied.

Of course he had moaned and raved to his parents about being forced to leave such a precious thing behind. His mother said, "Give it to me." She clutched it as if she would never let go and said, "I'll keep it for you till you make a friend over there who can come and collect it. That's my advice."

And so it happened that one day, a half year after Micha Zinochky left the Soviet Union, his mother received a letter from him asking her to bring a "little souvenir" to the lobby of the National Hotel in Moscow, where a "close friend" from Berlin would collect it.

2.

The person Micha Zinochky called "my friend" is actually one of Marya's employers, a young housewife working on a doctoral dissertation in literature. She has a comfortable lifestyle and impeccable liberal opinions. She hires her cleaning ladies with a heavy heart because she does not want to spoil herself, and she always makes friends with them. This soon leads to mutual disillusionment and inevitably a change of personnel.

Marya had only recently started work at Frau Christine's, as she calls her, and was already being asked to bring her husband

and daughter to dinner. Marya refused because she did not consider an employer suitable as a host.

When the fifth invitation was issued in a severe tone, implying that perhaps Marya was not bringing her family around because there was something wrong with them, Marya accepted an invitation to tea.

This occasion was marked by length—the Zinochkys came at three and stayed until midnight—and confusion about what should be eaten. Frau Christine loaded the table with food but did not once urge her guests to eat.

According to Russian rules of hospitality, a host must urge food on his guest until his will is broken. Frau Christine did nothing of the sort. She sensed her guests' shyness about eating, but was torn between a wish for her generosity to be honored and parsimony. This combined to make her hiccup half-finished sentences at them, "Take some . . . ," and then lapse into silence.

The Zinochkys did not eat more than the small helping of cake they found on their plates. Their daughter soon found the company dull and excused herself. She wandered around the flat, inspecting the adult toys there—the VCR, the books, the artworks—without envy, and then sat in a corner with a book while her parents chatted about shopping in the Soviet Union, a topic that gripped their host's interest because she was a great shopper herself.

The Zinochkys evidently expected Frau Christine's husband to appear at some point. It transpired after a few hours that he'd been home all along, a surly banker who had a football match to watch in his study. He entered, nodded at them, and, standing at the table, smeared himself a piece of bread and butter right in front of their famished eyes, afraid that if he took a seat he would have to talk to them.

After his retreat she made an effort to disband the party by yawning profusely and saying, "Well, well." The Zinochkys imitated her, yawned, said, "Well, well," smiled, and stayed on. Then they told Frau Christine about the ring.

Frau Christine was deeply shocked about the loss of their wedding rings. She offered at once to collect the remaining one the next time she went to the Soviet Union. She had never been before, that is, but why shouldn't she go? "I guess it's against the law, but what's the law? They can't bother me, I'm a citizen of a democracy!" she said. Ever since she discovered a certificate in the family attic that her mother had belonged to the Hitler Youth, Frau Christine had employed only Jews. She could think of no other way to repay what she considered to be her part of the German debt. Now an opportunity presented itself.

For the next few hours they planned how Frau Christine would save their wedding ring. At midnight she stood up and said, "It's been wonderful."

The ring was not mentioned again for a long time, but from that night on, Marya considered herself friends with her employer. Her work became shoddier. She regularly left ten minutes earlier than she should have, but she took sewing home with her and mended it in her spare time; that was friendship.

When Frau Christine's mother announced that she was going to Leningrad on holiday to visit the Hermitage, her daughter asked the elderly woman to make a side trip to Moscow to pick up the Zinochkys' wedding ring. She did not tell Frau Schmidt that the

Zinochkys were Jewish, fearing that she might then refuse. Frau Christine did not know her mother very well, nor, given the secret she had found in the attic, did she care to.

Frau Schmidt agreed. The Zinochkys were notified, their joy was really very touching. Then the old woman changed her mind, she didn't have the time to go to Moscow, and besides, she wasn't going to smuggle for a maid. Frau Christine berated her, "Go on, then, enjoy yourself in your museums." She had no choice but to go herself.

She planned the crime carefully. She heard that Russian trains were outrageously luxurious for the money and decided to travel by train. With her first-class ticket she found a customs declaration to fill out. It required the tourist to describe any jewelry taken into the Soviet Union. It stated expressly that only the items listed there, and nothing more, could be taken out again. Refusal to comply would be "taken seriously" by Soviet authorities. Frau Christine wrote, "One heavy gold ring."

Afterward, Frau Christine tripped to a cheap department store and picked out a large man's ring in gold-colored plastic. She expected the saleslady to recognize fraud: this dame is too fabulous to wear fakes, especially with a gland-size diamond on the other hand. The plastic ring took up half of Frau Christine's delicate finger. Next to it she wore the slender wedding ring she had chosen herself. "It looks like a fake if you wear it next to real gold," the saleslady suggested.

Frau Christine took off her wedding band and wore the plastic ring alone. It takes awhile to get used to a new constellation of rings on one's hand, and she did not want to draw attention to herself by any inadvertent tugging. Her husband did not notice that she was wearing a strange man's ring instead of her own. The new ring began to chip and lose gold at once. She turned the chipping portion inside toward her palm. She wasn't going to spend DM 7,95 twice.

She prepared for the journey publicly. She made a will so that their lawyer would know. She freshened up her inoculations so that her family doctor would know. She was sentimental toward her husband, cooked him his favorite dishes and made him promise not to be unfaithful in her absence because it would ruin the trust between them. She did not doubt her husband's fidelity, because the week she chose to travel was the European Cup finale; he would stay close to the television.

Frau Christine conducted a last meeting with the Zinochkys, this time at their apartment. Marya baked three different kinds of cake, and she heaped her guest's plate so full that Frau Christine was forced to be impolite and leave several servings untouched. Micha literally bounced around with excitement; he had bought himself Nike sneakers, which added to his height. He had a big package in his arms when he went to the door and he held on to it while he was showing her around the apartment. When they sat down for tea, he kept the package on the floor between his feet.

They discussed Frau Christine's meeting with Micha's parents. She would stand in the lobby of the National Hotel in Moscow holding a photograph of Micha. His parents would see the photo, nod, and, without giving any other sign of recognition, turn around and leave the hotel. They would wait in the entrance of a nearby subway station for Frau Christine to join them. They would go to a restaurant to talk. Frau Christine was to describe their Eden in Berlin, not forgetting the new bed and all the money they were earning.

Micha gave her the photo: it showed him opening presents in front of a Christmas tree.

When Frau Christine said she must be leaving, he took the package from between his feet, heaved it onto the table, and said, "This is for my parents."

Frau Christine complained that the package was too heavy. She could not carry it. She would have to pay a porter to carry it for her. She would not be able to lift it into the train or out of the luggage rack in her compartment. It was out of the question. Micha Zinochky was beside himself. "Oh please, please take it!" he cried. "The things inside will show them what the West is really about."

Frau Christine suggested a compromise. First she would pack her own luggage. Then she would add as many of Micha's presents as she could. The Zinochkys called a taxi for her and carried the package out to the street.

At home Frau Christine packed her Italian blue jeans and good pumps. Then she opened the Zinochkys' package and discovered two radios, a Walkman, Nescafé, a box of very cheap chocolates, an economy-size bottle of toilet cleaner, many rolls of toilet paper, and a bag of pastel-colored cotton wool balls. She took the box of chocolates and the cotton balls and left the rest behind.

The journey to Moscow was not luxurious. There was no such thing as first class, and Frau Christine had to share a compartment with two Polish women who spoke none of the civilized languages. This did not stop them from chattering away and sharing with her all the delicious snacks they had packed.

She began to wonder whether this might not be a foretaste of a Russian jail—there was no coffee, meals were served on tin plates, the public toilet was filthy, sleeping arrangements con-

sisted of bunk beds among strangers, there was no getting off
and nothing to do.

As they neared the border, the passengers fell silent. The porter paced up and down the corridor. Passengers placed their luggage in order. Frau Christine began to curse the fake gold ring on
her hand and the official paper in her passport that called it
"heavy gold." She couldn't change that now.

When the train pulled past the first shrubs of the border station, gray hats and uniforms stirred on the platform. The train
stopped and the border guards began to move swiftly—one
heard them mounting at the end of each car and begin to make
their way through each compartment.

Frau Christine could hear low officious voices and the answering tones of the passengers. Her Polish companions wrung
their hands. Finally the guards appeared in their doorway; they
had young, innocent faces and pale fingers that gripped her passport in an attentive way.

She tried to sit up straight on the cramped bottom bunk. Impossible. She crossed her legs anyway and ventured a smile.
White teeth were as rare as blue jeans in the East. But they
jerked their heads at each other and began to shout down the
train corridor. Their shouts were carried by others along the
quay, to an office in the station. They flicked her passport onto
the washstand, beckoned the Polish passengers into the next
compartment.

Now Frau Christine was all alone. Her passport was a bit
soapy. She rubbed it off with a damp cloth and looked at her
photo. Impulsively she nuzzled it—this could be good-bye. Then
she laid it back down on the sink, since this was apparently the
anointed place.

A while later two senior officials in business suits appeared in the doorway. They gave her the choice of four Western European languages. You choose, she replied, her hand dragging the fake gold through the air excitedly, French, English, German, as you like! They retrieved her passport from the sink, frowned because it was soapy, and said, German will probably be your native language.

They asked her about her visit, refusing to be drawn into her gayness, telling her to stay in her seat when she stood up to point out her cases on the luggage rack. They tore through them, removed all the guidebooks, and studied them. This is not very good, they said sadly, silly ideas about our country, before tossing them back into the suitcase. They checked her customs declaration.

A heavy gold ring?

Frau Christine trembled and extended her hand like her neck to the butcher.

They glanced at it hastily, as if embarrassment at what they were doing had set finally in, stamped the paper, and wished her a pleasant trip.

When Frau Christine arrived at the Hotel National in Moscow, the first thing she did was call home tearfully and tell her husband how glad she was that she was still all right and that soon, soon, she'd see him soon. She could hear the roar of the television soccer crowd in the background when he said, "That's good."

She changed into black. Black is for mourning. I've lost my innocence about the glamor of smuggling. Smuggling is merely frightening. And I look good in black. The lobby was full of important-looking men; from the looks and sounds of things, only influential men came to the East Bloc. One overheard conversations about cabinet posts and million-dollar contracts. Frau Christine began to like Russia. She passed the hairdresser's, where a manicure cost only thirty kopeks, one dollar, an extraordinary country.

The manicurist stared at the ring as she worked. She had never seen such a cheap ring on such a soft, wealthy hand before. While Frau Christine was on her way to the lobby, the manicurist described her client to her colleague. They had a good laugh: Germans! Probably she didn't know it was fake. There was gold dust on my towel after I finished, it was peeling all over the place, and the lady doesn't know it's fake. It's a tragedy really.

A comedy, said Frau Christine to a Mr. Adams in the lobby as she waited for Micha's parents. The American was waiting for a business partner, and she told him her story. The photo of the Zinochkys was in her shirt pocket, the bag of souvenirs in her purse, the plastic ring on her hand.

"You could get five years in Siberia for that," Mr. Adams said. "The Russians take their laws seriously, you know. If there is any way to back out, you should." He said good-bye with distaste.

The lobby was crowded. "Be inconspicuous," Micha had ordered. The husband of the maid giving orders! "Don't let anyone in the lobby see you meeting my parents." The nerve of him! She pushed through to the entrance, and then she recognized the fat elderly couple huddling uneasily at the door. The father was straining under a big package. She took out Micha's photograph, looked at it casually as she walked by them. They responded just as planned, nodding slightly, and as she returned the photo to her shirt pocket, the father turned around and walked out the front door.

But his wife did not follow him. She stood rooted to the spot, her face suddenly a mask of grief and horror. Then she burst into the loudest sobs Frau Christine had ever heard, sobs that riveted the attention of every person in the lobby and possibly some beyond. The lobby became absolutely silent, no one moved, nothing happened beyond the wailing of an old woman, in which slowly a word was discernible, the word *son*.

Then she fell into Frau Christine's arms, crushing the photograph.

Micha's father, waiting down in the subway station with his package, could hear his wife's sobbing as she came onto the platform, where human voices turn into trumpets. He looked away as she approached, but he did not scold his wife.

The elder Zinochkys then took Frau Christine on a long journey. They did not do the proper thing, tell her where they were going or pointing out any sights; they seemed indifferent to the beauty of the subway system or to the fact that a tourist might admire it. The stations flashed by until they got off without a word and began to walk. Micha's father stayed a few feet in front, his wife pointing at him from behind and tapping her forehead, saying, *"Verrückt,"* "crazy" in German. She repeated this until they reached a long line. At the head of the queue was a restaurant.

Ivan Zinochky pointed to the small medal he wore on his jacket as he made his way to the front of the line. Those waiting checked the medal and nodded their heads. Thus they entered the restaurant at once. A waiter greeted them respectfully and showed them to a table. The hall was filled with elderly men wearing the same medals as Zinochky, some decked out with dozens, their chests resembling a flower patch. The Zinochkys explained it was the anniversary of the end of the Great Patriotic War, what the capitalists still call World War II. On this occasion, veterans can eat in certain restaurants at the expense of the state.

A waiter deposited several platters on their table. Frau Christine hadn't eaten since morning and she took note of the steaming roast and potatoes, the caviar with eggs and salad, and the great hunks of fresh bread. But no sooner had she begun to enjoy this sight than tragic martial music started to play over a hidden loudspeaker. At once, cutlery clattered throughout the restaurant and everyone stood up. An impassioned voice addressed them over the music. The speaker remained invisible, while the food lay spread out before them.

No one seemed to object as the voice droned on. They concentrated. And then, one by one, the men took enormous handkerchiefs out of their jacket pockets and blew their noses. Some dabbed their eyes. Others allowed tears to stream down their large, wrinkled faces. The women reacted more slowly, but once their sorrow got started, it quickly gained strength until it outstripped that of the men. Only Frau Christine remained unmoved, trying desperately to ignore the hunger that had awoken in her like a beast at the smell of food. The speaker continued relentlessly. "He is reminding us of the comrades and relatives killed by the Germans," explained Ivan Zinochky, his eyes crimson.

"Give me the photo, please," asked Helena Zinochky. She held this with both hands and whimpered, "Son, son." This changed after awhile, became other nouns, ending finally in "ring, ring." Over the loudspeaker, the sermon continued.

The fake gold ring slid easily off Frau Christine's hand. She handed it to Ivan Zinochky, who looked at it, standing at attention, and his sobs turned to cackles. Helena wailed with the crowd and opened her own purse. She withdrew the wedding ring. Ivan Zinochky held the fake ring up to the light and laughed until he had to support his stomach. Then he crushed the plastic ring in his palm and dropped it into the caviar. Helena, awash, handed the wedding ring to Frau Christine, who tried to slip it onto her middle finger. It didn't fit. Micha was a small man, Frau Christine a large woman. She could fit it only on her wedding finger. As if she was married to Micha.

"You have brought us the radios, haven't you," said Helena, suddenly dry-eyed. "We'll sell them. We'll get a lot. Micha wanted that." Frau Christine fumbled inside her purse and retrieved the plastic bag with the chocolates and the cotton wool. Helena did not open it. She dropped it on her seat and said, "And I have something for you to take to him. Ivan. The box." Her husband shifted the heavy box along the floor with his feet till it reached Frau Christine's pumps.

Frau Christine stood in silence. "And this." Helen Zinochky reached into her purse and extracted a heavy silver goblet, which she placed on Frau Christine's empty plate. "I know he needs money. I don't believe him when he says he's working. Is he?" She didn't wait for a reply but added a pile of photos to Frau Christine's plate. The company was crying at hundreds of different pitches. Frau Christine thumbed through the photos. They showed Micha Zinochky with the girl he had wanted to marry. In one they hugged each other, clutching a square radio. Then the radio stood between them and they cavorted around it. The woman looked like a Ukrainian, with very high cheekbones. She wore a miniskirt that showed the expanse of her long, heavy legs, and leather boots.

"He adored her," said Helena Zinochky. "But she didn't want him."

She began to sob again, just as the speaker finished. The music changed to dance music. The men stuffed their soggy handkerchiefs back in their pockets and several headed for the dance floor at the back of the restaurant, where they began to fling their wives around. The Zinochkys sat down, moved the ingredients of Frau Christine's plate to her lap, and urged Frau Christine to eat. Eat she did, while her hosts did not touch the food, waiting for her to finish.

"I'll get into trouble," Frau Christine said after she had recovered her strength. "I can't smuggle this." Now Ivan stirred. He grabbed the silver goblet from Frau Christine's lap and sneered, "Trouble! For money. Money: bah!"

"You see, he's crazy, I told you so," cried Helena. "First he doesn't want to emigrate. Now this! The fact of the matter is, he doesn't want to live in Berlin because he doesn't want to be part of the Jewish community. I say, Look Ivan, look at this picture," she continued in German, her husband mumbling, "Money, *Geld, argent,* bah!" She pushed the photo of the Zinochkys under his nose. "Look, Look," she kept saying, "Micha with Marya in front of a Christmas tree. It's as good as here. No one makes them behave like Jews."

Back at the hotel, Frau Christine opened the box. It contained the most expensive Russian chocolate, aspirin, two rolls of cotton wool packed in plain paper, several books, and some Russian soap. She packed the cotton wool and one bar of chocolate.

She was determined to enjoy her stay in Moscow despite the danger ahead. But the next morning she was the victim of a terrible coincidence. In Red Square she ran into someone she knew: her mother.

Actually, Frau Christine was delighted to see her.

Mother and daughter spent the day shopping and sightseeing. Frau Schmidt did not once ask her daughter what she was doing in Moscow, and Frau Christine did not once ask her mother what *she* was doing in Moscow. And then, during an endless tour of the Kremlin, her mother recalled an adventure she'd had in 1938, when she was Christine's age.

Her friend, a certain Annie, had decided to emigrate to America. Frau Christine's mother, Ingrid, accompanied Annie to her boat in Bremerhaven, and just before she went through customs, the girls kissed good-bye. As they did so, Annie reached into her bosom and then dropped a diamond ring into her friend's hand. She said she had planned to smuggle it and was losing her nerve. Ingrid may as well keep it.

Then Annie passed through customs, where an inspector checked her person thoroughly before permitting her to board the waiting ship. On the gangway Annie turned and waved one last time. Then Ingrid broke through the police guard and ran up onto the gangway to embrace her friend. No one had the heart to stop them.

Frau Schmidt paused.

"What's the point of this story?" asked her daughter impatiently.

Frau Schmidt laughed. Then she said, "I don't know what

came over me. While I was hugging her, I slipped the ring into her pocket.''

Frau Christine arranged to fly back with her mother to Berlin. Frau Schmidt gave her daughter her own widow's ring to wear, which fit on Frau Christine's middle finger. Frau Schmidt wore the Zinochkys' wedding ring on her fat pinkie. When the customs inspector remarked about the size of the ring, Frau Schmidt said, ''Don't you worry your little head about it, sunshine.'' And he did not press the matter.

Frau Christine did not call the Zinochkys when she arrived home. When Marya came to clean, she gave her the package and the wedding ring and the picture of Micha with his first girlfriend as if it were a minor favor. Marya expressed her gratitude by cleaning up for an extra half hour. When she came the next day she reported that Micha had gotten so used to the melted-down half of a wedding ring he had worn west that he had decided to keep it. He had sold the large smuggled ring. It had fetched eighty marks. He was saving it for his car.

After she left, Frau Christine called the rabbi from the Jewish community and told him that it would no longer be necessary to give the Zinochkys money for Hanukkah, since they celebrated Christmas. The rabbi said, ''Eighty-five percent of my congregation isn't really Jewish. We can't be too fussy or we'd have no Jews at all.''

Frau Christine is left with a single consolation: if she leaves out the part with her mother, it makes a good story.

The

Doctor

Needs a

Home

She follows me, wherever I go. A ghost is not a being; it is a state of being.

Zesha has been in the women that come and go in my life, I have felt her warmth on their skins, her rapturous approval in their arousal, and when their demeanor turned cold, Zesha came to me and hated them for me, twice as much as I could. Recently two women have been unkind to me and Zesha is on the rampage. "Look at yourself! How handsome you are. Your beautiful thick hair, your strong face, your clever eyes. You're a bit stooped, though, sit up straight—head back. There. That's a man for you. Those geese don't know what they're turning down."

One of the women is named Barbara, she was my housekeeper. She is pretty as a picture, blond and voluptuous with a thrilling vulgarity of manner and speech—a Polish Madonna.

But Zesha disliked her for those reasons. Zesha was ethereal, even when she was of this earth. If people were vulgar, she withdrew into herself. Her deep-set eyes assumed a vacant look that I knew represented horror. Horror is what she felt toward Barbara. But when I held this fat Polish girl, reeking of small change and cheap candy, Zesha squirmed in my arms.

She is overjoyed because Barbara has left me, although the circumstances were sad: Barbara brought another man home. I found them in her bed, glued in and out to each other. Barbara became furious at my intrusion. Separating from her love (he was a simpleton, a Puerto Rican youth, her driving teacher) and standing up to her magnificent height, her baubles bouncing under my nose, she scooped me up the way Congress Poland dreamed of picking up Galicia and hurled me from one room to the next, my blood leaving its signature on the walls.

Then her driving teacher appeared. He had quietly put his clothes back on, a white suit. I must admit he had a decent appearance. When he saw what she was doing, he tried to restrain her. He shouted at her, "Leave the doctor alone!" I told myself: He is your friend.

The police tried to talk me out of my version of what had happened. They said, Are you a teddy bear? No woman could hurl you through two rooms. They arrested the driving teacher, Barbara packed her bags while I was giving my testimony, and by the time I'd finished, she had gone to her mother.

I needed Zesha's comfort and she dispensed it exuberantly in the hugs and kind words of a neighbor who cleaned up my walls and carpet with a special solution they sell nowadays to clean blood from furniture. So episodes like my quarrels with Barbara are apparently quite common. I am rather proud of it, in retrospect. It is the first real lovers' quarrel I've had. Life passed me by in that respect, partly because of my affection for Zesha, my sister, and partly because I am not the virile, muscular, potent sort of man they put in the movies. Zesha always said I was the only man in her life, but it didn't flatter me because it didn't alter the fact that I am rather frail, which counted against me. Yet women have always liked me for my brains—that has been a matter of luck for my body.

It turns out that the neighbor who cleans my walls is my daughter. She is pretty as a picture.

Zesha hates it when I comment on the physical features of a woman. She has been poisonous lately. Not because of the neighbor, who helps me out of the kindness of her heart. Zesha doesn't mind her because she means nothing to me. Zesha objects to Gretel, who visits me every Sunday and takes me to dinner. I look forward to this all week.

"Why? Does she do something for you?"

No, she does not *do* anything for me, although I think she used to. I have vague memories of Gretel trying to spend a night with me in the same bed, laying her head with its masses of hair on my chest and her arm across me, grabbing my far shoulder. I thought I was going to suffocate. I asked her to sleep on the living room sofa. I was tired, she offended.

I cannot remember her relationship to me. Perhaps we were married. I know I fell in love several times.

The first time I was five years old. The girl's name was Annula, she was seven years old and from a very important family —she was the baker's daughter. She lived on the other side of a wide body of water called the Hudson. The Hudson River separated my house from hers in Drohobyc. No—much more than a river separated our houses. Her father was a commanding figure, so unlike my short, hectic banker of a father; her mother tidy, mine book and music mad. Inside our house, maids strained to keep order. Inside Annula's, one smelled cabbage, holy water, and clean bedding. For a time I spent every afternoon after school holed up in Annula's kitchen, while Zesha moped at home. My mother didn't notice my absence, she was too busy reading or arguing with friends about some new idea she had.

Then Annula prepared for her Holy Communion, when even the most intelligent children turn into fanatics. She wanted to baptize me before my soul went to hell. The situation was urgent enough to justify a layman's baptism. One Sabbath afternoon I followed her into the warm, slimy water of the Hudson. We were up to our knees. "Deeper," she ordered. Her dress floated around her waist. "Deeper!" Finally, at shoulder level, she told me to dip my head underwater. She wanted to help; she held my head down for me. Afterward she said this was important. My head was large and Jewish and needed a heavy dosage of water. I could feel the humming of her chest as she chanted in Latin, and then I fought my beloved with everything I had. Finally I bit her on the hand and she released me.

I shot up all the way into the cold blue sky, and for an instant all remained as quiet as it had been underwater. Then the water trickled out of my ears, I could hear her laughing, and I could not stop fighting her, scratching, biting, and screaming.

My panic lasted for days. I thought: If I had almost died, death could still catch up with me; the days that had passed might prove an illusion. Death was too simple: a girl's hand like a pylon in the water. I realized that each breath I took was tenuous. Would there be another?

I waited, I counted. One day I didn't sleep and spent the entire day counting. That day I took 24,480 breaths. It seemed a wickedly even number: an average of 1,020 breaths an hour. If I hadn't been so excited, I might have taken exactly 1,000. The next day I counted the blinking of my eyes. But my eyes were devious, they wouldn't blink if they were being watched.

At an age when most people see their bodies as an ally, a source of joy, I had already identified mine as an enemy, even when it was apparently being good to me. And the evil force behind my body was nature.

That is why I became interested in science. I fell in love with nature the way one falls in love with a cold woman who rarely returns affection. I decided to devote my life to understanding her.

My darling Gretel keeps suggesting that I am disoriented. A ridiculous idea. I know perfectly well that we don't live in Drohobyc any longer, that we moved to Vienna because of Zesha and her talent.

At the same time that I settled on my vocation as a chemist, Zesha started to sing. She was a frail, red-haired child with pale brown eyes shaped like slits. Before she could talk, she hummed back any thread of music that passed her ears. As soon as she could toddle, she hung around the piano in the lounge, hoping someone would play. My mother knew a Chopin waltz in A-minor. She played it again and again, never varying its tempo or intonation, and the family members considered it background noise. Only Zesha took it seriously. At three, she suggested my mother should play it faster. The poor woman could not. She tried, got the notes mixed up, and Zesha clapped her hands over her ears and yowled with pain.

I do not wish to think badly about my mother. She was an

unblemished human being, a *Rabbinci*, the youngest child and cleverer than her five brothers. They delighted in her intellect and when no one was looking, taught her to read Hebrew. One day she snuck up behind her father in the temple and read aloud over his shoulder from the Torah; her father smacked her in front of everyone.

Her brothers laughed about this for many years. They went into business and politics; she married my father, a wealthy, good-natured, absent-minded bundle of nerves, who would tip his hat whenever he passed her on the street because he never recognized her. My mother followed her own interests, including the Chopin waltz. If she couldn't play the piano, that wasn't her fault. She took Zesha's talent to heart, made it her passion, and compensated fully for her own lack of repertoire by seeing to it that Zesha's was inexhaustible.

Zesha made her debut in Lemberg at seven. At eight she played in Vienna, and after that she was always surrounded by greedy-eyed, sweaty, hand-rubbing adults, including various famous pianists who wanted to keep a hand on her developing talent and on her pretty little person. She tolerated them quietly. She hated talking. She said, "Taking a breath and then moving your mouth, and pushing air up past your vocal cords—how exhausting!" My mother decided to move us all to Vienna; Drohobyc was too much of a backwater to contain a wunderkind's career.

I am oriented: I know that I live in New York now, and not in Vienna. And alas, life in New York is much more difficult than life in Vienna. The New Yorkers are proletariats, the Viennese petit bourgeoisie. That makes all the difference; because the petit bourgeoisie is more humane than the proletariat. In Vienna, Barbara would have been packed off to prison.

In Vienna, Zesha went from one fine gathering to another, giving concerts or just saying hello. Her performances received special notice because she was so pretty and yet so modest. I always remained her dearest friend, the only person in whom she took an interest at all. She never failed to ask what I was doing, applauding my progress, and making a note of who my own friends were. She once said to me, "I love to listen to you talk, it is like music to me."

But one day, when she was sixteen, Zesha complained, "Music no longer speaks to me."

She didn't want to practice. She circled around the piano like a dog forced to pass an enemy. "You'll never have a career that way!" my mother scolded. Zesha never commented. She retired to a chair in the lounge and wouldn't leave it on her own.

She stopped eating. She became limp and light as a dead butterfly. She followed me around with her crooked eyes that said: Kiss me, Stach, my dear brother. Hold me and kiss me as you always did when I was younger. And then she did not look at me anymore.

She was diagnosed a schizophrenic by Freud when she was seventeen, analyzed by Adler at eighteen and nineteen (no use! no use!), in an institution for the insane at twenty, deaf and lame at twenty-two.

Even when Zesha no longer spoke to anyone, she was always with me. She encouraged me in the laboratory, she held me when I embraced Katinka, the daughter of the baker next to the opera. Katinka's kisses were O-shaped and tasted of whipped cream. In the evenings, I visited her at the warm, sweet-smelling ovens. One sensation flowed into the next, we ate fresh *Apfel-*

strudel and then kissed again, and in between she nudged the conversation around to religion. Like Annula, she wanted to baptize me. I thought of Zesha: disapproval.

I changed coffeehouses and met Giedonka. She was a red-haired cabaret singer, and pretty as a picture. She lived in Budapest, but whenever she had an engagement in Vienna she wrote me a note and I met her at the train station, no matter how late at night, to carry her bags and pay for the taxi to her hotel. In return for this I was allowed to drink brandy with her after her performances. This went on, until one night I mustered the courage to invite her out the next afternoon. She agreed. Zesha's face: excitement.

In daylight I saw my Giedonka had something on her mouth that she covered with an extra dab of lipstick. I noticed this while we shared an ice cream, eating from one spoon. I could not eat anymore. The mouth I had planned to kiss for so many weeks, whose warmth I had felt, now repelled me. Nothing to do about it but excuse myself.

I do not need Zesha to remind me about the danger of kissing. I was forced to study medicine because chemistry was considered the domain of the physician. The sight of blood made me queasy. Naked bodies made me dizzy; I fainted when I saw a corpse. Zesha was with me when I received my title, Doctor of Medicine, the only graduate who had not even a rudimentary knowledge of anatomy.

I haven't missed knowing about anatomy for a minute. In the first place, no woman acceptable to my parents wanted me. Science is an art, not a profession. Other parents warn their daughters not to have anything to do with a scientist—they are unreliable, eccentric, and self-indulgent. My father indulged me to the hilt, he paid for my laboratory and for an assistant, so I never had to worry about earning a living at all.

That was before hoodlums overran the country and killed him. My sister and my mother went east, back to Galicia, and I went west: a simple equation that equals separation. But I have managed without them, and without my father's money. The Americans immediately paid me a salary for my work, and they made me a professor, although the proletariat doesn't consider this a very prestigious post. But other professors respect me because I've received many prizes. There was one in particular, very noble, that everyone wanted. Zesha was with me when it dropped into my hand under very hot, bright lights. I do not know what I have done with it. I used to have it in my desk. But what has become of my desk? No doubt someone has stolen it, used the wood for their fireplace and had the metal melted down.

I admit I have problems since my housekeeper left, but I beg you to understand—my problems have nothing to do with aging. Old age has not affected me yet. If I just indulged in a long passage all in the past tense, I did this deliberately, and not because I forgot how to use the present tense, as some old people do. Of course, one practically forbids me the use of the future tense! But I will use it presently.

I will use it the next time I see Gretel. My darling reminds me of Annula, she is taller and heavier than me and has the aura of deeply felt Christianity that I've always admired. We were allied in some way once, apparently through carelessness.

It happened after a party. Severo was there, and Erwin, and

Hans. They did not have their prizes yet, they were commoners. I was already a nobleman. Gretel was one of the few girls there, she had a light, pleasant Austrian accent and was pretty as a picture. Her parents had left Salzburg after the war and she was studying to become a pathologist, that was her life's dream but everyone found that hilarious, a young, lithe pathologist. Salvadore kept playing with his tie in a suggestive way and Gretel giggled incessantly. Her teeth were big but her eyes were even bigger, huge and blue, they were not like Zesha's little eyes at all, and she was rather husky, while Zesha was always tiny. Gretel looked like the Virgin, strong and with sky blue eyes. And then I played Holy Ghost.

I remember the scene we had when she told me she was expecting a child. I said, "For heaven's sake!" in a disgusted way. She held that against me. A few years later she told me it had caused irreparable damage, a knife into her affections, even though in the next breath I asked her to marry me.

I was shocked that she didn't turn me down. She said she wanted to think about it. She asked me to meet her at Times Square at 2:00 P.M. She would give me her answer. Then she went to my laboratory without my permission and took a vat of Brassica arvensis. She poured this into the bathtub of her dingy walk-up apartment. She didn't have a penny then, she was doing her residency in that vile profession. My Madonna made herself a bath bright and hot enough to make blood turn on itself. She sat in it for a half hour, toweled herself off, and hiked 150 blocks to meet me. We went to a Horn and Hardart, she excused herself to use the ladies' room, checked to see if there were any results, and, since there were none, she came out and said, "OK, I'll marry you."

She didn't tell her father because he would have killed her. He was a typical Austrian medical man; he didn't want an intellectual in the family.

I have a chat with Gretel.

Me: "I believe in the absolute value of human life, that there is life without a body, a purely spiritual life. And that this life is unbelievably complex. Nature has no business there at all."

Gretel: "Listen, I have to go, what do you want?"

Me: "I have to admit that communication with Zesha was never a matter of speech. So the fact that her body is not here with me is not relevant. That is the high level on which I meet her. You and I meet on the sea bottom of daily life."

Gretel: "Can I call you back?"

I am not used to waiting for people to call me back, and so I quickly get impatient. This weakness is the first sign of aging in me, although I cannot deny that nature has defeated me in one other respect: she has allowed me to turn ninety years old in a visible way (even if intellectually she has not touched a hair on me).

Me: "I realize this number—ninety—which applies to me, matters to you. You are that superficial, my dear."

Gretel: "Stach, I am going to hang up now."

Me: "Of course I am rather critical of how women look. And women over eighty are seldom attractive—that is the great tragedy in the life of a very old man."

Gretel: "Good-bye."

And so I must now face the question, Why doesn't Gretel call back?

Gretel inhabits a villa on the other shore of the Danube. She shares this with her father, an ancient, wrathful invalid. There is another figure that occupies the villa, a housekeeper they brought with them, along with all of their furniture, the crucifixes, and the first of a dynasty of dachshunds. This servant is their most precious possession, all day long she rushes around to serve them, cooking the Wagnerian dishes they are used to. Her face is the most ferocious in the family, but they commonly refer to her as a saint, because she has sacrificed her life for them instead of for a husband.

One of her most important tasks is keeping me out of the house. During the day she stands guard at the phone. No matter how often I call, I can't wear her down. I've tried, believe me. The number is such a pleasure to dial: 201-927-3969. A lyrical number, the telephone of a beautiful woman.

But then it is the Saint who answers: "Residence Dr. Umpfenbach." Dr. Umpfenbach referring to the father, a pathologist, as well as to his pathologist daughter. The original Dr. Umpfenbach is no longer professionally active, these days he works as a watchdog who makes sure that I do not approach his daughter. His job is to insist that she is not there, to stomp up to the phone, snatch it out of the Saint's hand, accuse her loudly of incompetence, and then take over the job personally, "You can come here on Sunday afternoon. Please don't call us anymore, and leave Gretel in peace—you're no longer married to her, thank God!"

He is not necessarily lying about his daughter. I have taken a taxi to her villa and looked for Gretel under the beds and established that she was really not there. "At work! At work!" the old man shrieked at me. "She is working at the morgue!" I have waited behind a bush for her to return at night, followed her up the front steps, and witnessed how she brought him all her spare devotion.

I have concluded: This is where I feel happiest, among Austrians, good Austrians. The Teutonic people always understood the Jews better than the Jews could understand themselves. I herewith invite any Austrian to visit me in my laboratory. I will take the time to show him around. My laboratory is at the university hospital. But non-Austrians are welcome too.

Oh—you do not know where it is! Well, then. I will tell you: You take the big road leading out of the square in Drohobyc, with the kosher butcher at the corner. The road runs along the river to a great bridge. Cross that and keep going until you reach the Dairy Queen. A left, then a right. See the roses? See the statue of the dachshund? This house is friendly to dachshunds. The master of the house is called Happy, he is twenty centimeters tall, and his tail flails like a saber.

Oh, but now I have led you to Gretel's. What duplicity. But let's go in, as we've come all this way. I will show you where I spend the finest hours of the week, my Sunday afternoons, underneath that dangerous chandelier, seated, as guest of honor at the gleaming dining room table. I am their sacrifice. On Sunday, fresh from confession and communion, they must be nice to me. The Saint serves me schnitzel, *Ochsenfleisch, Mehlspeisen.* Nobody talks. Well-bred Austrians do not speak at the dinner table. However, it is easy to stir up conversation. All I have to do is taint the silence with a verb set into the future tense. Then all three put down their forks and ask me whether I have sorted out my life, now that the housekeeper is gone: What are you going to do with yourself?

"You should be in a place where you are looked after, a good home is what you need, we can find you one, you have enough money," urges Gretel.

"A professor's salary," sneers Dr. Umpfenbach.

"Where you won't need to call us on the telephone all the time," trills the Saint.

I smile politely and wait for dessert. *Palatschinken? Quarkstrudel?* I agree with them completely, and I have a home in mind: right here. I hope to stay forever, I am willing to call Dr. Umpfenbach "Papa." Suddenly Gretel gets nervous and tells me about our daughter, but I would rather eat some more dessert and then retire to the guest room. It suits me perfectly, and it is next to Gretel's bedroom. I have managed to reach it and drunk the odor of clean bedding and holy water. At night the mahogany bed ends shine in the dark, illuminating the portraits of various prestigious ancestors, all pathologists. I will be watched over by a family of dissectors. Zesha will mope here, but she'll get used to it. Will will will.

"Be sensible," they shriek, fluttering around me, pecking and clawing. "You can't sleep here! We can't look after you! Get a new housekeeper!" Gretel is hailing a taxi while the Saint and Dr. Umpfenbach force me into a big coat and then position themselves on each side of me, helping me down the front steps. I manage to scramble back up again, my canes clatter down to the sidewalk, and the two ancients rattle after me and collar me.

Yes, I adore it there. I have put aside my bachelor days. I would like to live there forever after.

Ever since I expressed my desire to move to the far side of the Danube and take part in an orderly, petit bourgeois existence, Gretel keeps harping on her plan for me to retire from the university and move into what she calls "a home," which is an institution for the weak and demented. I would like to point out that this is impossible, since I still have important work to do.

The university is only a short walk from my apartment. I negotiate this fluently, in the elegant walking shoes Gretel gave me for Christmas. She wanted to prove she still cares for me, so she bought me the finest brand, called Sneakers. My daily visits to the laboratory are essential or the technicians will start to laze around. Everyone greets me with the utmost respect, they say, "Hello, Doctor," to me there, some, "Hi there, Junior."

I settle down at my desk. Later I go to my coffeehouse. This is a pleasant, clean place with excellent *Apfelstrudel,* and no one objects if I read the newspaper. There are lots of other regular guests, mostly Negroes. The Negroes replace the Jews in this particular café. They are much quieter as guests, though.

This coffeehouse is a kind of investment for me. I collect the plastic silverware and cardboard trays and use them at home. I have enough napkins to serve cocktail snacks to all the members of the academy. The napkins say McDonald's on them, which is funny. Because the Dr. McDonald who won the prize in chemistry in 1942 will think they are his, and that I have stolen them from him, which I haven't. I have merely collected them in a clever way, taking always two napkins instead of one at the till and then pocketing the extra one. For a while I used them for toilet paper, which saved me a lot of money. Now I take toilet paper from the university and save the napkins for the academy.

Today a terrible thing happened, and I am beside myself. I was sitting quietly at the laboratory when a technician swept by me and said, "Well, Doctor, how's it feel to sit at your former desk?"

I don't know what she meant by "former." A tremble ran from my head down to my feet. "Former, you say! What does that mean?"

I believe I was then involved in a commotion. I may have slapped her. I hope I did, because she deserved it. Then a man appeared. He was very strong, the way Americans often are. He held me very tightly until I relaxed in his arms.

Then he turned to the others who were clucking around us and addressed them in a deep voice. He told them something worrisome that I didn't know, that I am not well. I understand that I suffer from ulcer of the *Heimat*. I'm sure he called it "ulcheimers."

"Write it down, I don't believe it," I told him, "I will ask a specialist," and he laughed and he wrote down "Alzheimer's disease."

"But you're very old," he said. "It can happen at your age." He said this in such a friendly way that I chose not to argue with him.

He brought me home, turned on the television for me, and spoke with great deference to me. "Make yourself comfortable now, stay at home for a while. Someone is going to have to look after you."

I watched some television and then I began to miss Gretel. At once Zesha objected, "That goose wants nothing to do with you, save your strength for important things." But I put Zesha out of my mind and dialed that most precious of all telephone numbers, 201-927-3969.

They did not want to let me speak to Gretel. The Saint said, "Gretel is too tired to talk to you, and it is too late to call."

"This is outrageous. I want to talk to her!"

She hung up. I called right back and said I would come and

see her, I could spend the night under one blanket with the dachshund, if that made them feel better, I was prepared, and I didn't mind the old pathologist at all.

The Saint shrieked, "No! Don't you dare!"

And then Gretel came to the phone, her voice tired and old, and said, "Stach, please, be reasonable, and let us get some sleep, it is two in the morning."

"Be reasonable! What is reasonable—leaving me here all alone?"

She hung up the phone. I dialed again. It rang forever and even though I shouted, "Gretel, Gretel!" she did not answer.

So I put on my Sneakers shoes and walked back through a cold, bright night to the university. It was very crowded. All my colleagues were there, in the same shape as I was, wanting a word with someone. We sat around together, all night long, discussing the meaning of life. Toward morning a pretty woman sat down and asked me who I was, and whether I was emotionally attached, or even married. She wanted to know before becoming friendly with me and getting her hopes up. I assured her my marriage to Gretel was over, but she was suspicious. She wanted to call Gretel herself.

It turns out she only wanted to complain about me. She claims I was making a nuisance of myself in the hospital emergency room. Gretel was outraged that everyone should hold her responsible for me, just because of a short-lived marriage survived by one child.

I am all alone today, alone with my devious body.

Alone with Zesha's voice breathing in and out of my ears, her heartbeat beating next to mine, Zesha, my darling, old age stole up on me suddenly, I am ill and alone. My face is cold. For an hour my eyes produce tears, for no reason. Then they stop. Now my face feels stretched and dry. An itch runs down one arm, hops to my chest, to my big toe. There it burrows. I sit all day hunched over the itch in my toe. The toe turns blue.

In the evening a woman comes in and unbends me. She has soft hands but she is too wrinkled to be pretty. Her face is wet. "Dry your face, whoever you are."

I tell her, "You are about to drip on me."

She replies, "Look at your toe!"

She kneels before me, holding my foot carefully, as if it were precious. I quite like her, and she looks most familiar to me. Could she be my sister?

She laughs at this. "I'm your daughter."

"Then who is your mother?"

"Gretel is my mother," she says, "but don't worry about it."

"It's not important," I say.

"Don't scratch anymore, you fool!" she screams.

She helped me to bed and attached the telephone to her ear. She knew how to put her finger in the little holes and turn them until someone talked to her. I have forgotten how to do that.

While I was thinking about all this, she disappeared. I checked my silverware. It was gone. And my money! Every penny.

So she was a thief. She took everything, I hadn't a penny left, my prize was stolen ages ago. I tried to telephone the police. My finger fit into the last of the holes steady and firm, there, and with a mighty swoop it turned the wheel all the way.

My finger was stuck, having gone too far under the silver

bridge, but I wrestled myself free. The telephone fang marks were deep and I dreaded the consequences, gangrene, amputation. Then a friendly voice called me through the receiver, "Operating."

The policeman was tall and handsome, an American man, he reminded me of Severo when he collected his prize. Joining the ranks of the noblemen. I thought I would faint from admiration. To be tall, handsome, Christian, and a brilliant scientist. There are some very small, ugly non-Christians among us, you know. And then a handsome knight like Severo.

Severo fought for the Republic. When someone disturbed him, he shot off his head. Me, I never squashed an insect. I went to France and when my enemy followed me to France, then I hopped a boat to America.

I left my mother with Zesha. My sister started talking again when our mother stopped. Our mother stopped from one minute to the next after our father died. A life that had been devoted to the opening and shutting of her mouth was suddenly reduced to silence as she watched her husband's body lowered into the ground. God's decision. Let there be peace! Zesha had been allowed out of the hospital for the burial. No sooner was our mother quiet than Zesha awoke out of her trance. She pushed her wheelchair away from the cemetery.

I was impatient to leave Austria. I bought Zesha two train tickets back to Drohobyc. I said, Take Mama back, and wait for me to send for you from New York. I brought them to the train station. They waved at me through the window. That is, Zesha held Mama's hand and flapped it for her. The wind peeled Zesha's red hair back off her sweet, pale face. My mother's face was vacant, as if no one was home.

I haven't heard from them in a long time. I am beginning to lose hope that they are alive.

That's the problem. No one visits me. Not even Severo or Hans or Sarcastic Erwin. I call up Gretel and cry to her that they haven't visited me in years!

She corrects me. I gave a cocktail party last year. Everyone came. But I behaved badly. "You invite them for cocktails and forget to buy drinks, and then, while everyone is standing around politely trying to talk, you turn on the television full volume and sit down to watch 'All in the Family.' "

That's a lie! That never happened. I will call Severo and Hans and Erwin and ask them to recount the episode for me. But my telephone is busy. Ah, yes, the policeman is using it, he is talking to someone. I demand to know who, after all, it is my telephone, and he says, "Your daughter." Then he turns his back to me and stage whispers into the telephone, "Christ, lady, you got one problem here."

> *Day, night.*
> *Dark, light.*
> *Hot, cold.*
> *Hungry, full.*

What's the difference between them? The difference exists, I admit. But it is not significant. "Eat something!" cries my neighbor.

I did not know I had such a pretty neighbor. "You haven't eaten in weeks by the look of you, we must do something about you."

Then she changes her mind and screams, "You've just

eaten breakfast! Aren't you full? Don't tell me you want to eat again."

Later, "I've made you breakfast five times in a row. Now you wait for a few hours and then you'll have lunch."

And then she says something very very sad. "And after lunch I'll have to go."

"Where's Gretel?" I ask.

"Gretel and you aren't married anymore. You deserted her. Listen, she has her own life now. Leave her alone. Once a week she'll see you. Out of the goodness of her heart!"

"You're all the same rot!" I cry.

"Good-bye," she says. She kisses my cheek. She has tears in her eyes. I wish I could remember who she is, although it doesn't make any difference.

Then I suddenly wake up: "My *Schwester*!"

Kuss, I say.

Speak English! she says.

Kuss, Kuss, Schwesterchen.

I follow her, she walks away. I grab her and kiss her forehead. That's how I like it. No diseases that way. Live forever kissing that way.

Strong this morning. I remember how to use the telephone. I call the number anchored in my memory, 201-927-3969, and tell the woman who answers in a weary voice that Zesha hates her from her Christian insides to her coarse Christian skin.

This woman—who is she, how does she know anything?— tells me, "Listen, your sister isn't around, get it through your head, you were a bastard to her, you sent her home to

Drohobyc, remember, when the Nazis came. You only looked out for yourself. An egocentric artist. The Nazis shot her, and your mother, and threw them into a ditch."

Hubbub with the hot blue light, what do you call it: gas. I have left the gas stove on again. They smelled it. They burst into my apartment and danced around me like baboons shouting: Ovens are danes, they are ages, you must light them. With these things. They wave little sticks at me and strike them, and then there is fire everywhere. They are writing a long list of all the things I do wrong.

A man is kinder to me than the rest. Now, Doctor, don't run around barefoot here in the halls, go back to your own apartment. He brings me there. "Watch your television, and leave the cooking to the lady who comes."

Tonight on television a good pogrom.

I want to be with Gretel, and she says, "No, you cannot come."

"Why not? I am well. I can stomach the sounds and smells of aging in the home, I am not ashamed of seeing the decay of your parents."

"It is my family who objects to you. Because you are a bother," she replies.

"Your bother, my darling, that makes you my sister."

After all these years the hoodlums are still trying to catch up with me. Or am I suffering an illusion? The boat to America, Gretel, the prize, all illusions?

To teach everyone a lesson, I turn the gas stove on again without lighting it. Suddenly a woman walks in the door. I take her in my arms, and she doesn't resist. She is a husky, pretty woman. I cry a little, it has been such a long time since I've held someone. "I don't know what our relationship is but I know we are close, please tell me that we are related."

"Let us pack you a bag," she says. "We are taking you to a home. It's all arranged. My cab is waiting downstairs."

I can fling my fears and ambition to the wind. I have reached an age where the word *home* means everything to me. I can say, as every normal man does upon receiving the news while on military duty, or in prison, At last, at last I am going home, in this case to the villa on the Danube where I belong. And like a normal man—life passed me by in this respect—I am frantic with joy.

Mr. Lustgarten Falls in Love

When the maid moved in with him, Mr. Lustgarten thought, Didn't Goethe also fall in love with a young woman? He began to think of himself as very much in love. His relations had hired Anna Kaminska sight unseen. Instead of traveling all the way from Boston and New Haven down to New York (in the snow), his sons called the Catholic parish and asked the priest whether he knew anyone who could look after their old father. They described him proudly and apologetically—an ex-intellectual, author of several volumes published in Austria before the war, who had build up a catering service at a good downtown address. No, no, he was not Catholic, but he had married one and allowed her to raise the children outside of his own faith. Now he was widowed and in his grief (an irreplaceable mother) doddering gently without getting aggressive about it. He needed someone competent and reliable to live in and provide basic care. No, not a companion. A maid. The Lustgarten sons took turns on the phone. Expense was no issue. He had the money, but he would not pay for it; they would pay for it. (Hidden costs or complications never occurred to them.)

"I have someone with a good character," offered the priest, "you know: honest, punctual. There's only one problem. She's Polish. Some people don't like that. There's suddenly such a lot of them."

"Perfect!" said Mr. Lustgarten's children without reflection. "That's what he speaks sometimes."

Mr. Lustgarten was born in the 1890s somewhere in Austria-Hungary, where the finer small-town people pretended they were living in Prussia. The boy's parents spoke a polished German, his nannies a vulgar Polish, and he treated both as equals. Lustgarten left home to study, and while he was gone Austria-Hungary disappeared.

Over the next two decades, Lustgarten changed his residencies and citizenships with the same nonchalance with which he grew older. He landed in New York harbor in 1941 with a half-empty suitcase and no family left, but he was the master of several trades, and they were his wealth; he was never afraid of America the way some of the European refugees were.

Old age surprised him suddenly, like a defection of the servants, running out with his faculties. He could no longer keep order among time and events. Then speech began slipping from his memory in the reverse order that he had acquired it: English was the first to go, then Portuguese, then French, then Ukrainian, ancient Greek and Latin fell away as one; German stood a long test and then failed, leaving only the Polish his parents had disdained.

"It's part of the problem," conceded his sons. "Imagine. He speaks Polish indiscriminately to everyone, at the store, on the streets, even to us!" They had all been born in the United States to a Brooklyn-bred mother. They had the American openmind-edness about foreign labor and the fear of foreign languages.

So, one winter morning Anna Kaminska rang the doorbell of his increasingly shabby upper Broadway apartment and simply introduced herself. She rang three times before the neighboring door opened a slit and an old lady's voice peeped out, "You want him to answer, you gotta call first. The telephone he hears—there's a pay phone on the corner."

Mr. Lustgarten always answered his telephone vigorously, like this: "Hallawww!" But he answered the door shyly. He was intimidated not by his own physical infirmity—he had always been frail—but by his poor memory. He was thrilled at the sight of a real lady, crooking his head sideways and up to get a better look. At the same time he was remembering that the predominant features of his own face were jowls, wrinkles, and crow's feet. But he remembered too the keenness one had attributed to his eyes, the intelligent melancholiness of his smile. He kept his fluffy white hair well groomed and always wore a clean shirt and tie with his faded trousers and ramshackle bedroom slippers. He still thought of himself as a gentleman. "Excuse me, do I know you?" he asked Anna Kaminska. So he isn't completely gaga yet, his neighbor thought, spying through the door slit; what luck for him to get a visitor.

He had been right not to recognize her. Mr. Lustgarten welcomed her by turning around and shuffling down the hall. At the far end, newspaper leaves were fluttering up and down like pigeons in a loft. There was a snowy draft. "May I close the window?" asked Anna Kaminska, following him.

"I have just been throwing out the garbage," Mr. Lustgarten explained.

Anna Kaminska stayed, moving into the small maid's room

with its own bath at the far end of Mr. Lustgarten's large, disheveled apartment. The old man noticed but did not object when she threw out all the old newspapers into the garbage bins. Later he realized that she had disposed of the paper bags he kept for dire emergencies in his closet; but he accepted her judgment as one of female metaphysics, even if they made no sense economically. He respected her for never allowing him in her room or in the kitchen. Indeed, he adored the way she shooed him away when she was cooking—how she turned around from the stove or sink, her bright nylon skirts twirling, and how her red cheeks would puff out and the red mouth pucker to expel those lovely words, "Pan Lustgarten!" He cultivated a naughty expression and a way of backing off mischievously. That he had aroused her seemed proof of his vitality. Besides, Anna Kaminska did not force any significant changes on him. She did not insist, as his children had tried to do, that he move his bed out of the dining room. Instead she moved the dining room table into the master bedroom. Just as Mrs. Lustgarten had done, the Polish maid tidied the apartment, cooked him simple meals, and took his laundry to the Laundromat. When she threw out his shabby house slippers and bought him new ones in the same style, Mr. Lustgarten felt that Goethe would understand his emotions exactly.

In short, Mr. Lustgarten recognized in Anna Kaminska—in her gestures and acts—the quintessence of womanhood as he had always longed for it. It did not matter to him that she was much taller and stronger than he; when they sat down together at the dinner table they were the same height. Then he had to fight down the impulse to stroke her red hair, worn in an old-fashioned bouffant, which he now found to be the prettiest style women had ever worn. He would run his fingers over her white freckled neck or along her soft white hands if he were not such a gentleman. At my age? he laughed to himself proudly.

While Mr. Lustgarten did not know anything more about Anna Kaminska than he saw and felt, he was neither curious nor mistrustful. They lived together, and what he recognized was her presence and the absence of his loneliness. Mr. Lustgarten no longer called his sons to complain about their indecency for leaving him somehow so alone. Now when Mr. Lustgarten's children called him, he always seemed so pleasantly surprised to hear their voices. Once he had answered every query with bitterness. Now he replied, "Oh, me? I'm fine, fine. But how are *you*?" This unnerved his children. "And how is Mrs. Kaminska working out?" they asked leadingly.

"I don't think she's a 'Mrs.' You mean my friend Anna?" he replied, as though it were a strange question. "Well, I guess she's fine too. She seems very happy with me."

Soon their filial curiosity turned to deep concern. "How old is she?" they asked casually. "What does she look like?"

"Very young," he boasted, "very pretty. A redhead, as they say here. Too young for me, unfortunately, nineteen or twenty years, she told me once, I forget. I'm a very old man, you know. Otherwise . . . !" And he giggled with satisfaction. "But don't worry. Don't think that I have a liaison with her." He loved the sound of that word, *liaison.*

One day when they called, he remarked, "You mustn't be worried that I will marry her. Your inheritance is secure."

No sooner had this come rather thoughtlessly out of his mouth than it occurred to him: Well, and why not? You're an old man, admit it! he told himself fiercely. Goethe was too, he rejoined.

"Anna, my darling," he ventured afterward, toddling after her into the kitchen. "Are you married by any chance? I am just curious."

"Out of the kitchen," she replied. "Yes, I am," she told him later, after he asked again. Her voice indicated no emotion to him. "My husband lives in Poland." Although Mr. Lustgarten had just now thought of marrying her, this obstacle to happiness deeply shocked him. Now, for the first time, he became curious about her, about her past, her present, and her plans. He was too discreet to ask the really important questions directly. "Probably your husband loves you very much," he said. "And you him!" Then he turned away before she could answer, afraid to hear her say yes.

He began to put other questions to her with more hopes of an answer. "Where were you the other afternoon?" he asked.

"Shopping for a blouse," she replied.

"Where do you go when you go out during the evening?" he ventured.

"To church," she said, "to Mass. Last week there was a bazaar." She answered his questions promptly and with a brevity that he felt at first came from modesty—that she did not find herself interesting. Soon he would suspect other motives. She also volunteered that she had come from Poland two years earlier for reasons she did not volunteer and that she had lived in the parish home for refugees, taking care of the priest's sewing and washing. Did she speak with a touch too much veneration of this priest? worried Mr. Lustgarten. He did not dare ask whether she had any other friends in the parish.

"Who is your husband, Anna?"

"Tadeusz Kaminsky, Pan Lustgarten. A pharmacist."

"Do you have children?"

"No."

"Well, you are still very young, you still can. Are you going out again this evening?"

"No. But I am always back by ten o'clock when I do go out."

Mr. Lustgarten began to notice when her tone was irritated.

Mr. Lustgarten's children had presumed that at the price they were paying the Polish maid, she could also be ordered, if necessary, to keep her distance from their father emotionally, so they did not worry overly much about his enthusiasm for her. They did, however, mention the financial arrangement to him. A great deal of money. A maid, in their employ. Mr. Lustgarten ignored these remarks. "She is nice to me because she is happy with me. She is my friend. A lonely young woman. She had some troubles with her husband, I suppose." He did not think she was working for him. What was there to do, anyway? He was not some sort of incontinent old man!

But he became more and more mistrustful of her. Her absences preoccupied him. There must be someone outside there who was interested in her. Or was it possible that she was interested in someone else, another man? Unthinkable! Soon Mr. Lustgarten forced himself to face the question: What if his Anna should fall in love with someone else? Inevitably other men would notice her white skin, her red hair, her femininity. And she must know it, because before she left to go out by herself, she invariably teased her hair into perfect place, and put a dab of perfume behind her lovely ears, and straightened out her colorful skirts. When he saw her looking into a mirror, his heart ached. Her vanity appalled him. Would she kindly leave her telephone number, then? She complied. If he did not misplace the number, then he called it within minutes of her leaving the house. The parish church answered. "Just for emergencies!" Anna Kaminska scolded him later. He felt her cold and insensitive then. "And please don't phone on Sundays, because they won't call me out of a crowded mass!"

On Sundays his suffering was almost intolerable.

His children usually called him on Sunday mornings (the cheaper rates) and increasingly he answered the telephone in a terrible temper. "Hallaawww! What do you want?"

"What is the matter?" they begged.

"Nothing!" he snapped. "Nothing is the matter. I have some small troubles with people you don't know." But finally one Sunday his agony made him reckless and he admitted, "She is cruel to me."

Their gravest suspicions confirmed, Mr. Lustgarten's children all called him one after the other to pry, "What does she do to you?" But he refused to elaborate. So they were left to fitful speculation. Never had they worried so much about their "poor old father." One had heard, of course, about the savageries servants committed when their ancient employers became helpless. "I cannot tell you what she does. It is too painful for me to talk about it," said Mr. Lustgarten in a broken voice. "Yes, yes, a miserable tormentor."

At this admission, Mr. Lustgarten's children agreed that the time had come to intervene. They tried in vain to reach the parish priest who had recommended this Mrs. Kaminska, but he had some sort of new upstate telephone number. In the parish office no one could say anything helpful about her beyond that she must be one of the ones from Poland; there were quite a few. Mr. Lustgarten's children conferred and decided to invite the old man up to Boston and New Haven for a week, respectively, rather than having one of the family drive all the way down to New York (in the heat).

He arrived, dragging a suitcase so thoughtfully packed that only a woman could have managed that. "She was glad to see me go!" he cried. After spending two days in Boston and three days in New Haven pacing about the telephone or dialing his home number to see whether she was home (she generally was; the conversation was in Polish), he bolted back to New York, where, in his first call back to his sons, he choked with unhappiness at how she "treated" him—it was Sunday morning.

Mr. Lustgarten's children saw that they were now treading the dangerous ground of negligence, that if their father was merely annoying them now, he could haunt them later. They had unwittingly placed him in the hands of a ruthless young opportunist, beautiful and without sympathy for the aged. And although it was really a great inconvenience, they organized a joint trip down to New York (in the pleasant Indian summer), coming in a posse of three four-door air-conditioned compacts that gained speed steadily with anxiety at what they might find, reaching the poor neighborhood with a screech of wheels and no patience to find legal parking spaces. They met in the lobby of their father's building, summoned up family spirit to rush up the stairs (elevator out of order), a band of the righteous: three sons with wallets bulging in their hip pockets, blast of the doorbell, the neighbor appearing with, "Ya gotta call first, even if he's not alone," but then the door opened and it must be she:

Anna Kaminska, a woman of perhaps fifty years with a lot of white in her doudy red bouffant hairdo, frail despite her corpulence, with a simple, swollen face, little dull blue eyes, a rosary worming its way through her fingers. "Oh!" she said in alarm.

Mr. Lustgarten shuffled up behind her with an absentminded, thoroughly contented expression. "Oh, hallaw!" he said. Then he welcomed them in, as a prince to his palace. Anna Kaminska disappeared into the kitchen to make coffee and arrange little homemade cakes, which she sat down on the dining room table in the bedroom before retreating tactfully into her own little room, where they visited her each by turn, among the crucifixes and holy water, religious books, and photos of nephews, nieces, puppies, and dried flowers, herself a shy picture of isolation and piety. Self-sacrificing and therefore eminently deserving.

Mr. Lustgarten's children were deeply humbled.

"Father, you just don't know your own luck!" they chastised him angrily. From then on they would not tolerate another ominous word about her. Instead they raised her salary, and behind her back they blessed her.

And the next year, when Mr. Lustgarten turned ninety, they gave a dinner for him in New Haven where she was invited. They begged her to sit at his right hand like a bride and, knowing that as a good Catholic she would never give her husband safely estranged back in Poland a divorce, they asked if they could call her Mama.

*L*etters

from a

*F*ather

Right up to the second of March, 1944, Dr. Nagel, a remote, stern town doctor, liked to complain that his hothearted son Laszlo was a stranger to him. It had always been like that, he said: Laszlo had no talent for moderation. Moved by his own words, Dr. Nagel sighed and patted his grandson Peter on the head.

Dr. Nagel's rakish-looking son had made a local girl pregnant when she was seventeen. At eighteen she bore him a son, at twenty, a daughter. When she was twenty-three years old, Laszlo Nagel drove his wife to her death in his new car. He escaped with bumps and scratches on his handsome exterior.

He felt sad for a while but he could not change his nature; he adored being alive. He was a merry widower. When he was offered a diplomatic post in Berlin, his father protested that it would be dangerous for a Jew there, Hungarian or not. His son Laszlo responded, "Nonsense. I'm a good-luck man." He took his children with him.

Peter and Celina settled down with their father in the German capital. They lived in a beautiful villa with extensive gardens. They walked to school, and when they returned at noon, Annie Schmitt, a good-natured Catholic girl from the Rhineland, looked after them. Laszlo Nagel loved his children and always found time to play with them, any sort of delightful nonsense. In the evenings he was generally gone, but it became an iron-clad ritual every morning that the children crept into his bedroom and breakfasted on top of the bed covers with him and whomever else happened to have spent the night there—sometimes women, sometimes men. It was a jolly time.

After the Kristallnacht in 1938, Laszlo Nagel said, "I'm a good-luck man. But you children haven't proven yourselves in this respect." He said this regretfully, and then he had tears in his eyes. They gathered force and spurted over his cheeks, something that often happened to him during a bout of heavy laughing. The children thought perhaps his words were some sort of difficult joke.

Annie Schmitt took Celina back to her village on the Rhine, introduced her there as Lise Schmitt, her daughter out of wedlock. The scandal soon blew over. Peter was dispatched back to the small town on the Austro-Hungarian border where his grandfather presided. He hadn't wanted to leave. He was already seven years old, but he had had a tantrum when his father and the chauffeur called him from the frosty garden and showed him a packed suitcase in the hall. The chauffeur had left the car turned on and panting in front of the door in order to hurry the procedure. Peter had hurled himself around the hall beneath his father's gaze, breaking the hall mirror. "That will bring you good luck," his father said. Then the boy broke a vase. "That's bad luck," his father said.

The father picked his son up, kissed him from top to bottom, repeated a hundred times that he loved him, and made the following proposition. "You write to me once a week, and I'll write to you at least once a week. That way we'll stay together."

His grandfather's house was a fiefdom of visitors and servants, bound by respect for the owner and ruled by the clock. House ceremony insured that life was continuous, no calamity could upset the order of things: breakfast at 7:00, a ceremonial dinner at 1:00 P.M., high tea in the library at 5:00, and a light supper at 8:00. Dr. Nagel was technically retired as physician but he continued to treat patients, receiving them every morning in his office on the ground floor. He dispensed drugs very rarely. His principle medication was a kind of gruff promise that nothing serious was the matter, nothing that time wouldn't heal.

Every Saturday, without fail, a letter from Peter's father would arrive. Peter always spent Saturday morning perched on the high stone wall surrounding the house. From there he could see the mailman as he approached their street corner. As soon as he spotted him, he sprang down from the wall and raced toward him. His grandfather didn't allow the postman to hand out the mail to his grandson. "I've got something for you," the mailman said. "You have to wait." The boy accompanied him back to the house, watched while the mailman handed his letter over to a maid, who brought it to his grandfather's study. At high tea that afternoon, the letter was lying on the library table and Dr. Nagel gave Peter permission to pick it up and open it.

Laszlo Nagel's handwriting began neatly at the top of the page —he never had any trouble deciphering the "Dearest Most Beloved Son"—thereafter his writing settled into a slant, as if words were pouring downward, until his letter became an illegible splashing. If Peter asked his grandfather for help, the old man made a disapproving face, but he read it aloud to him. "One can always read one's son's handwriting," he remarked, "no matter how much of a stranger he is."

The letters were long, cheerful descriptions of the city, the parties, the ladies and gentlemen of Berlin society. They always promised a reunion as soon as the situation allowed it, and foresaw in fact that the situation was improving, because, after all, "I'm a good-luck man and don't you forget it." The letters unfailingly closed with happy outbursts of affection for his son.

All week long Peter worked on his replies, trying to make them equally witty, just as cheerful, even if he didn't feel the slightest bit cheerful or witty. Peter wrote to Laszlo Nagel about town life, about the guests his grandfather had, about school, which he disliked, being a moderately interested pupil, about the old family wolfhound and the multitude of neighborhood cats that he called his best friends.

And his father wrote back exuberant, happy letters, with those invectives of tenderness at the end that his grandfather refused to read aloud because they were so foreign to him, so immoderate. "And this part you can make out yourself, it is between you and your father," he sniffed. He never ever said an overly nice word to anyone; Peter could not imagine he ever had.

He was not drawn to his grandfather, he was put off by the skin that was rough as bark on his face and hands, the lichenlike mustache, his smell of toilet water, disinfectant, and tobacco. But he respected him, as everyone did. Dr. Nagel always knew best. He was a physician, after all. Dr. Nagel was also kind. He never turned down anyone looking for help. He hadn't written a bill for his services in years. But if Peter had ever wanted to be cuddled by that huge, stiff figure, his grandfather would surely not have managed such a gesture. When forced by circumstances of the heart to say something tender, he remarked in an offhanded way, "I'm fond of you, you know." And that was it.

Peter's childhood seemed to be passing in this interim situation. In three years nothing had changed. Germany had gone to war, but the arrangements in Dr. Nagel's house made politics seem powerless. Breakfast, lunch, tea, and dinner, those were the laws. And the boundaries that mattered were drawn in the house. Peter had his own large, sunny room, but he knew the clean, narrow rooms of the cooks and the maids equally well. He never entered the formal living room without being invited, or the library, where he might be asked for afternoon tea. His grandfather's study was no more than a closed door to him, the room behind it entirely off limits, even more so than his grandfather's bedroom, where he was sometimes called in, just for a minute, to see some family heirloom stored in one of the huge wardrobes. The garden was divided into territory that he could visit: the lawn, the little woods at the back, and an off-bounds area: the fruit trees, the vegetable patch. The chauffeur's house down the street was part of Peter's terrain, and the gardener's apartment three blocks away, where he was always welcome.

Peter might have been very lonely if his father had not stuck to his word and written him faithfully in his ghastly scrawl. And even the scrawl improved one day, when a letter arrived that was typed and he could understand every word. From then on he did not once need to ask his grandfather for assistance, and his father's letters were his alone. "You haven't been the only one to suffer under my handwriting," his father wrote, explaining that a close friend had given him a typewriter for his birthday, although it was hard to find typewriters now, even in Berlin, because of the war. "This office machinery is just another piece of luck," wrote Laszlo Nagel to his son, and signed off with one hundred fatherly kisses that did not embarrass him because they were typed, so his grandfather did not even have to see them.

It happened one late summer afternoon, when Peter was already eleven years old, that the house felt different. He had eaten breakfast with his grandfather and gone to school, returning for lunch as usual. Lunch had proceeded normally. Afterward he had gone out to visit the dog. He heard the car in the driveway but did not ask himself who was coming or going. When he returned to the house it was in the grip of a silence much more pervasive than when his grandfather was napping. Peter heard noises in the kitchen and found the cook at her business. Dr. Nagel, she said, has gone to visit your aunt in Budapest. He would be back by nightfall.

Without the danger of running into his grandfather, Peter Nagel wandered around the house, drifting inexorably toward the areas where he was not allowed. He felt himself swept on a current of curiosity toward his grandfather's study.

The heavy brass door handle was placed high up on the door, at Peter's shoulder level. He could hang on it, with all of his weight, and then it might budge. Since the door was certainly locked, he thought, there could be no harm in trying. The door handle went down. The door opened.

From the doorway he saw a huge dark desk over at a window that overlooked the back garden. Bookshelves stood along the opposite wall. One shelf was lined with bottles. Inside the bottles he could see floating objects that looked like dolls. Bottled dolls. He took one step inside, and when this did not cause him to be struck at once by a bolt of lightning, he took another step. And then another. The bottles contained very tiny naked babies. On another shelf stood more bottles, these with odd pieces of flesh that looked like ordinary but ancient butcher meat. The smell was peculiar, sour. The other shelves were full of dark, heavy books that looked like Bibles, but when he pulled several out and opened them, they proved to have gruesome illustrations of various kinds of sickness and sick people. He stopped every so often and trained his ears toward the door. The grasshoppers droned in the backyard bushes. Presumably he would hear the car returning. He relaxed and resumed his investigation. Against another wall was a chest with dozens of drawers, each holding tablets of different colors and sizes. On the desk next to the typewriter stood a glass half full of gold liquid. He sniffed at the glass: alcohol. He pulled open a desk drawer. Pens, pencils, desk supplies. He pulled open another drawer. Paper, in all different sizes and colors. He slid open yet another drawer and found a plain box.

He stopped to listen for a car. Nothing. Then he pulled the box out, opened it. It was nearly bursting with folded pages. Letters. He removed the top one and was confused. He recognized his own handwriting. They were letters he had written to his father. He pawed through them, forgetting their order, stirring them up. He glanced at them, each word a slash of embarrassment. What silliness he had written. And his grandfather had read them all!

All of his anecdotes, his false cheer. He replaced them and looked back into the drawer. There was another box, and inside that another collection of his own letters to his father. Now something was dawning on him.

He looked back at the typewriter. A piece of paper was wound around the roll and had several lines typed on it. It was a letter that began, "Dearest Most Beloved Son!"

He went on writing to his father, in the same cheerful tone. He made a fool of himself knowingly now. He read his father's letters, trying to feel the same delight at the cheery news, at the affection he never had from his grandfather. What else could he do? He could not admit to Dr. Nagel that he had prowled in his study. And he did not have the courage to ask about the truth.

The situation was changing anyway. Anxiety lay in the air. At the chauffeur's house someone said the Germans were coming. Soon people said it openly in the kitchen at home. When Dr. Nagel heard the help speaking about the Germans, he was angry. He went into the kitchen and he said, "Time will heal it. Stop worrying about the Nazis. The Nazis are not coming. I know what I am talking about." Since he had always and invariably known what he was talking about, the staff was ashamed: for a while they believed him.

Then the whispering began again. The Germans are coming. Laszlo is in trouble, Laszlo conspired. This time Dr. Nagel confronted them individually. He went into the kitchen to see the cook, he went outside to the garage to see the chauffeur, to the garden to see the gardener. "Listen," he demanded. "Stop this foolish chatter. I'm an old man and I can't stand it. As a physician, I understand something of the ways of the world, do I not?"

They agreed that he did.

"And so you can believe me when I tell you, as a physician: the Germans are not coming."

And again they relaxed, they believed him. He was the town doctor. Anyway, it was Christmas. But by the end of February, the rumors began again. The town was just five miles from the Austrian border. It would be the first to go. The Germans are coming, Laszlo conspired, he made false passports for Jews, he's been executed.

On the second of March, 1944, Dr. Nagel went to the bank. When he returned, he had lunch as usual. After lunch he had the staff assemble around his dining table. He invited the neighbors as well. He poured everyone a sherry. The table was crowded, the way it had been in the heyday of his family, when his children were still at home. "The Germans are not coming," he said. "I know. And in order to prove it, I am going to pay out six months of wages ahead of time. Would I do that if the Germans were coming?"

And solemnly, the way he did everything, he passed out envelopes. Inside each envelope was a large wad of money, exactly the sum that he owed for six months of work. After he had extracted a promise from each in turn that he could now have his peace and quiet for six months from their gooselike fear, he retired to his study, as he always did after lunch.

The butler had prepared a little speech of thanks that he was going to administer at teatime that afternoon—the table was set in the library. But Dr. Nagel was not punctual. After a half hour had passed, the tea was cold. The butler called Peter and said,

"Go knock on your grandfather's door and remind him that it's teatime."

Peter knocked. He felt the stabbing of his bad conscience every time he passed the study. When his grandfather did not respond, he fetched the butler, and the butler knocked, and when there was no response, he fetched the cook, and she knocked. The cook went in. She found Dr. Nagel slumped at his desk, his head on the typewriter, covering the page he had written, his arms dangling. Peering in from the threshold, Peter watched the cook's hand travel to the old man's shoulder and then yank away, her head tip back slowly, her mouth inch open, her eyes begin to bulge. A strange wobbling up her neck evidently carried the scream that tore at last the interminable quiet of the doctor's home.

When the undertaker came for Dr. Nagel, he glanced at the last words of the deceased in the typewriter and wondered a little.

> My Dearest Most Beloved Son,
> Spring has finally made it to the north.

"Bad luck," he grumbled, as he always did. His profession had not inured him to a feeling of outrage about death. Perhaps it was really good luck. The next day, the Germans came.

An Aesthetic

Compromise

of Small

Importance

There is no earthly reason, they say, not to live *well*. For the price of a car—and Gunther Neutz already denies himself a car—you can have beautiful interiors. He had some sort of leftist antipathies to them when, at thirty-five, he married away from his mother's traditional tenement. But his wife Margaret had newly converted to the belief in stable marriage with sacrifices one called compromises, and she insisted on surroundings that suit a still-young leftist academic couple. Aesthetic judgments are universal, people say. If Gunther could not always be counted on to respond to her looks (the blond hair, fine complexion, and pretty features are not unusual and subject to alteration), then surely he would to the Picasso litho. If not to her wealthy family in Wuppertal, then certainly, despite his political convictions, to the Biedermeier furniture she inherited from an aunt.

Margaret Neutz designed their apartment in an old Berlin building, zealously observing the local intelligentsia's opinion that high stucco ceilings should be reflected in polished parquet floors, that the asymmetry of the *Berliner Zimmer* should be accentuated, not hidden by a calculated placing of a perfect old German furniture piece. The Neutzes' white-carpeted bedroom lies behind a pair of sliding doors, with a broad white eiderdown over a slender mahogany bed frame, an altar to the rituals of monogamy. "But I don't want any children," stated Gunther Neutz categorically.

Certain kinds of monogamy are explicitly childless. It is another aesthetic question resolved and there are no cats as substitutes. Having no children bestows a wealth of quiet on a couple, blesses them with the multiplicity of their own interests. At the Neutzes', friends leave an occasional imprint, usually in the form of good books displayed on a teak table in the living-room. The house owner intruded recently to renovate the bathroom with chrome fixtures that are stylistically alien but unquestionably comfortable. Nor do the cosmetics stationed there imply an aesthetic compromise of any importance, not even the bombs of glycerin stored in the refrigerator next to the truffles. Otherwise the way the space is lived in represents only the finest opinions: Bunzlau china is charming, anemones should never be arranged with greens, flowers go in pots, not on furniture coverings, *Jugendstil* and long-necked standing lamps from Milan have form, curtains should be white and walls chamois, hidden stay the hands of the once-a-week housekeeper one shamefacedly engaged and then enthusiastically kept, the subject of a telephone number handed around at proscuitto and melon parties, who does her work creatively, they say.

Too bad, they continue, it is obviously all wasted on Neutz. His wife tolerates his absentmindedness, his comical abstemiousness, that he works too much, wolfs down her best cutlets without appreciation, never dances at parties, and drinks no wine at all. Relies on the name beneath the doorbell to recognize his own home.

In fact, Gunther Neutz is not all indifferent to gracious living. To the contrary, Neutz is even more sentimental about interiors than most. Only he doesn't know it yet. Until a certain episode, Gunther Neutz believes that any interest he takes in a room beyond the warmth and shelter it gives proves his good-natured tolerance of Margaret's folly. He has always refused to discuss Tuscany with her. Privately, he battles any frivolous thoughts by pretending they didn't happen. Sometimes he looks in the mirror and notices his reflection with pleasant surprise: there he is, funny how easily one forgets the blond hair, round blue eyes, hawk nose, bit of an elongated skull, that's Aryan. When threatened by idleness, he looks for his reflection somewhere. If he can't find it, then he silently recites poetry he memorized as a boy. When he has exhausted his repertoire, he sorts molecules into configurations he likes. Neutz is good with atoms, he puts them to novel use in anthropology. He teaches in a Thuringian accent that has driven the sensitive to switch fields. No mime ability: a kind of honesty. He's quaint for the eighties, sentimental about the human race. His mother had him for the Führer in a *Lebensborn Haus;* all he knows about his father are his head measurements. He knows more about himself: why, there I am, Gunther Zeuss Neutz, heading along a sunny street on an honorable assignment. Neutz promised a student to mail her a book but he became so engrossed in his work that he forgot to ask his secretary. Now he is atoning for his negligence by delivering the book in person. Neutz has his principles. Even if he is a tenured professor, he fulfills every university duty he can.

His student, a Frau Khan, lives at 76 Kolner Strasse. Passing numbers 22 and 24, he looks for himself leaping out of shop windows, a stooping stick figure with a canine face. The street becomes residential.

"He who dares to circle the flame becomes the flame's satellite." Number 32, number 36.

"It seemed the sky had kissed the earth to sleep." At last. Press: Khan c/o Schmidt. Sublets. No elevator. Neutz enters a dark stairwell and begins to climb, his sandals flip-flopping at each step. By the time he reaches the third floor, he is rather interested in the adventure. He can hardly remember what Frau Khan looks like. Asian, obviously. Third world. On the fifth floor the stairwell branches into two doors: KHAN C/O SCHMIDT and WC. He rings and steps back, considering for the first time that she might be surprised. The door opens at once to a dismal light reflecting off a bare gray floor, and a small figure in the middle who says, "Oh, Professor Neutz!" at the book he is gallantly extending.

"Forgot to mail this, silly of me, you wouldn't have had it all weekend," he says, his feet turned back toward the stairs, his thin shoulder pointing like a setter at the open door.

"You want to come in for a minute?" she says.

He thinks for a moment, steps inside. Doesn't actually mind seeing other apartments, the furnishings, the paintings on the wall; wife always delivers a commentary later. Did you see the Chinese runner? Always hope nothing from Ikea if you already like someone. Interiors tell you everything.

But where's the furniture? Frau Khan boils water for tea at a hotplate on the windowsill, turning her back so that he can concentrate on the scant square of a room, green wallpaper rising out of a shiny gray-painted floor, a low green ceiling overhead.

Two small slanted windows are propped open, through which the room gasps for air. The furniture exists, of course. An air-filled mattress you could take to the beach, an Appollinaris box, queen of table waters, as a coffee table. Against another wall, more boxes are neatly stacked on their sides and filled with books and clothing. A naked light bulb not turned on is taped to the wall by its cord just above the bed, at the level of Neutz's knees. By the time Frau Khan has poured water over tea bags suspended in a white Melitta coffee pot, he notices a blond, chubby juvenile with a cheerful pink-and-white face. Khan? Her name could be Gretchen. "What's your name?" he asks, smiling lopsidedly. "Gerda," she says faintly. Her hands tremble pouring the tea into matching Melitta cups.

Sitting on the floor like a boy, resting his elbows on the Appollinaris box, Professor Neutz gulps black tea to the pounding of his heart. The painted gray floorboards! The green papered walls! Grimy-fingered evening poking through the curtainless window! Everything's immaculate, three hooks nailed into one wall hold coats and dresses. The pillow end pokes out of its blue-and-white-striped pillow case with a price tag stilled stapled there, DM 19,90. The books sorted into boxes! As the room darkens, she talks about the newest evolutionary theory from America, and he barely listens. That is why she talks. The famous Professor Neutz drinking tea with me and getting bored and wishing to go, terrible; she tries desperately to impress him with her fine mind.

Abruptly he stands up over her to leave. She stands up too, sadly, to see him out. "Monday you lecture about genetics?" she asks, bending to switch on that bedside light. As this ignites, dousing them with the purest yellow bulb light, Gunther Neutz can no longer contain his passion, and exposes it.

Dear Gunther has been more absentminded than usual. Walks

around with two different-color socks showing through the sandals he always wears after the first of May. He works harder than ever, will work himself sick, boasts Margaret. He arrives punctually to dinner parties only if colleagues or members of the press are invited.

In fact, Neutz is infused with vitality. When he looks into the hall mirror on his way out at dawn to see his Frau Khan, he sees a little boy there, with naughty blue eyes, a red mouth, blond curls. *Be good!* he hears his mother's voice. And he speeds out the door. Every single workday morning he flip-flops up the stairs of 76 Kolner Strasse, Gerda Khan hears him and opens the door in advance. When he first sees her smiling at him, he suffers a stab of bad conscience and unpleasant surprise that makes him frown. But this changes into a grin of self-effacing desire at the look of that recklessly bare room, with green wallpaper and low ceilings and slipshod furnishings and the brazen tastelessness of the Melitta coffee set. While she washes up a bit in the tiny porcelain sink, he undresses carefully, folding his clothes into a little pile, and then he lies down to wait for her in the only possible place. They hardly speak. If anyone speaks, he does. Tells her how much he has to do. She asks him questions about his work. She doesn't dare breach any other topic. She is just twenty, honored by the early morning visits of famous Professor Neutz. 1A on the civil servant scale. Donates his money to left-wing causes and cancer research. She doesn't ever ask about the wife she knows he has from rumors. He always talks in the first person singular about everything. "I went to Rome last year. . . ." "I live. . . ." "I have a friend . . . ," and so on. She attends his lectures religiously. But as before, he always disappears very quickly afterward, doesn't even say hello to her. If occasionally his gaze fixes on her absentmindedly as a member of the first row, then she flushes with pride, certain that everyone notices.

But one day she risks exposing their acquaintance. At his closing "Thank you," Gerda Khan springs impulsively to his side. "Well, what are you doing here?" he asks her pleasantly, and they walk out of the lecture room together. "Oh, going for a walk," she replies. "Maybe with you." And her face turns red with fear of having gone too far. But he only chuckles magnanimously, and they proceed, together! How everyone must be staring! Then an old woman stops him, ignoring the girl absolutely, "Gunther, I've been trying to reach you. . . ." Gerda Khan frowns at the wrinkles on her forehead, at her heavy stomach. An older woman, she thinks with great bitterness. For the first time she recognizes her own value. Encouraged, she coaxes Neutz away by saying, "Good-bye, Gunther" and turning aside. Scarcely out of the door, he catches up with her and she presses against him in public, gladly offering him her youth. Professor Neutz accepts. He props his arm around her shoulder, but his gait is suddenly so hasty, his arm so stiff and heavy, that she panics and asks him about the next day's lecture. "Yes, I have to prepare it," replies Neutz, "so much to do," and he disengages. "But maybe we can go for a walk somewhere else soon."

Gunther Zeuss Neutz bolting home by subway, amazed at the ease of his own gesture—that he placed his arm around a pretty girl on a pretty day, like any young man. When he was young he never did this. For seven years he had a relationship with a Neukoln woman fifteen years older than he, with two children and an indifferent but jealous husband. She had thrown herself at him when he was eighteen and ordering his lunch at the Karstadt cafeteria during final examinations. He had glimpsed her at the head of the line, a face in the steam, and then his tray sped down the sparkling counter until he stood before her mutely, suddenly acutely aware of the smell of hot, clean porcelain, the romance of alpine tables and benches. Then came her smile and the stretching of her short arm to hand him his sausage. He remembered the glint of her wedding ring and the shine of the five red fingernails, the gold watch, and the smooth upper arm with a dimpled inoculation scar, "Hello Sweetie." During the next seven years he hungered for the few minutes he had with her by flashlight in the dry cellar of her apartment building, among the children's bicycles, their skis, the table one didn't want just now, and an old discarded mattress.

Years later, when Margaret took him over, she had to teach him the rudimentaries of romantic behavior: the use of certain phrases and gestures, the transsubstantiation when one undressed, the symbolism of a soft, clean bed. Gradually he gave up his queer habits, although he reverted at night to sleep utterly on his own; on his side with his long, lean legs drawn up in the newborn's position.

Margaret counted her blessings. At least he declared his love, in a charming old-fashioned tongue *("You inflame me")*. And even if he never took the slightest interest in her personally, he accepted her as his wife. There is never a lack of admirers for the wife of a famous man, especially one who does not work at the relationship. Everyone could see he was much too busy. Monogamy takes two. One expected her to seek companionship— Gunther wouldn't know the difference.

Gunther, just coming home now through the wooden door with the art deco glass panel in the middle, presses the valuable antique handle gently. But at the same time he is wondering whether he couldn't, in fact, take the girl somewhere, this Gerda, third world but doesn't look it, on a long walk, or a little trip. Honeymoon, young man in love, pretty girl, that's how it's done.

"Have I told you that I have to go to Hamburg tomorrow? I have to see Professor Hochmann," he remarks to his wife, who is cooking dinner and doesn't register the vagueness of his voice over the din of frying her schnitzels. "Important." He never considers that the girl may not want to go. He'll pay her way, of course. Some fund will receive that much less next month. "You'll spend the night in the usual place?" she asks. Of course. The hotel the university always used. He hadn't even thought about that, how thoughtful of Margaret; he pats her shoulder.

The next morning Neutz packs his pinstriped pajamas in his briefcase among several books and leaves noisily in new oxfords. He plods down the darkened Kolner Strasse to Khan c/o Schmidt, thunders up the stairs, wheezes at the sight of the pink sky in the little slanted windows, yellow glow of the bulb, the four bare, dark corners, the startled, sleepy girl pleased to see him any time. "I'm going to Hamburg. Do you want to come?"

Of course she does. She pulls a pair of underpants from a Bulgarian canned tomatoes box. An innate sense of order, I hadn't noticed, he marvels. And off they go. They read magazines on the plane, not looking at each other. Hamburg takes just a minute. Then they take the bus to the hotel, checking in as Herr and Frau Neutz.

"Madame," the porter mocks the girl. The elevator. Is this

way. *The corridor begins here.* And here is your room, modernized, with all the refinements of Wilhelmine bedroom furniture. Natural light seeps in through the net curtains. Gunther Neutz pulls the heavy purple curtains shut romantically and then stumbles around looking for a light switch. Finally he grasps the copper-based bedside lamp.

Frau and Herr Neutz smile timidly and undress, folding their clothes neatly. Gerda has learned exactly the habit he learned from his wife, who picked it up from a French soldier whose favorite phrase was "Let me explain." They sidle into bed with the cramped speed that comes from sudden anxiety. Because what's this? Gunther Neutz has no desire. None. Who's this girl? He fights for orientation and sees only his own face in the base of one bedside lamp, twisted and stretched and yellowing. "Khan, Gerda" he mumbles. All around the walls towering, the curtains plunging, the sparkling chandelier. Gunther extinguishes the light. The feel of eiderdown and fresh sheets reminds him of his mother. He sniffs and smells only the slightly sweaty girl. "Let's try a more natural position," he says. He clamors out of bed on all fours, the girl following. Then, panting, they wrench the mattress off the bed and tug it laboriously into an empty corner, the sheets tangling. They open the curtains, rip off the sheets altogether, and lie down on the bare mattress, the genuine horsehair label under their noses. Gunther concentrates on the bare walls and the smell of the corner. There's a fingerful of dirt there. No use. Gerda Khan is getting frantic. Forbidden by the unspoken rules to ask him personal questions, she dares a compromise. "What's the matter?"

But before this breach of good taste must be answered, the telephone rings harshly. Professor Hochmann. "Professor Neutz, how delighted I am to hear you've finally come to see me." Professor Neutz: "I'm just on my way now." Sniffles from the girl are muffled by the corner. She can go look at the town. "I'll be back tonight," he promises.

He will be very tired tonight. Too tired. Too tired in general for this affair. She will drop his seminar. "Poor Miss Khan," he will think to himself nostalgically on future mornings when he remains lying next to the familiar sacred heap of his wife. "How fortunate I am to have a beautiful home." And the white curtains move in mysterious ways to indicate agreement as just then a draft enters the room, carries a bank statement from a small desk through the open double doors over the bare parquet along the walls, brushing the Picasso and then back, the blue-and-white slip swirling in the splendor of the quiet, childless rooms that circle the marital bed.

*S*trange

*T*raffic

Charles Is Noticed

When the dark-haired, nondescript accountant from Oregon first stepped onto German concrete at Frankfurt Airport, he made the following gesture: the index and middle fingers of his right hand grazed his forehead, slid down to his chest, and flapped over the left, then the right side of his rib cage.

At once the trouble began. As he collected his baggage and asked about transferring to an inland flight to Berlin, people gawked. It was a mistake to speak German. He was immediately noticed. The baggage clerk had seen his American passport and bedlam broke out among his prejudices. "Oh, you're not German. But your German is so good. Why is your German so good?"

"It's not good at all, many mistakes, my parents were German." Charles Allen had trouble lying.

"Aha." The clerk concentrated. "And when did your parents leave Germany?"

"1955."

"The flight to Berlin leaves from gate four," the clerk said, suspecting he had been fooled.

"Your German is flawless. When did your family leave Germany?" asked Charles Allen's neighbor on the flight to Berlin. The American looked past him, through the window at the clouds and replied, "1950."

"So you say you're an American—and I say impossible! They can't learn foreign languages," cried the taxi-driver, swerving the steering wheel in consternation.

"My parents were German," Mr. Allen explained in his deep, unsteady voice. And so it went.

His interrogators were suspicious. It seemed to Allen that only politeness prevented them from pouncing and tearing him into bleeding pieces: "When did they leave Germany?" they snarled. "1945" implied that his parents had been good comrades who knew when to leave. The answer "1955" meant they were unpatriotic opportunists, turning their backs for economic reasons, pitiable in view of the current weakness of the dollar and the low, two percent inflation in the *Heimat.*

But not everyone was gullible. The taxi-driver, steering absentmindedly along the Kurfürstendamm to the Pension Central remarked, "Your German is much too good for an American. You must be very smart."

And of course cleverness is the classic giveaway.

Charles Gives Himself Advice

Do not behave cleverly. Read your newspaper alone in the dowdy *Pension* dining-room. Do not talk to the concierge who has seen your passport unless absolutely necessary. Speak English, even with the other steady lodger, Herr Nadler, who understands only German. Concentrate on speaking English without any accent, R's belong in the trough of your mouth and not rattling at the back of your throat. Smile often. Wash behind your ears, polish your loafers. Admit to nothing.

Charles Runs Out of Advice

Possibly because he was not home in Athens, Oregon, the Dodgers had lost three consecutive games, and the Yankees were looking better every day. There was a hot spell in Central Europe. Two weeks passed, during which he ignored the business matter that had brought him to Berlin.

Instead he led the life of the *Pension*. He took all of his meals with Herr Nadler, his neighbor, a permanent guest. He found eating anything other than sweets a task, but when he had been good and completed his meal then he rewarded himself with a sensual act: reading the sports page of an American newspaper while lying on his bed.

For a few hours every afternoon he ventured outside dressed in his national colors, a red tie, white shirt, and blue trousers and jacket. He only visited places and restaurants mentioned in his tourbook. He kept a business letter in the front pocket of his pants, as though he might actually see to his business. The envelope's sharp edges pricked his groin. He tugged at it and the old women of Berlin glared at him.

He returned home in the evenings to watch the unsatisfactory German sports games on the television in the lounge until he was tired enough to sleep. In this way he spent the last days of summer.

Then the seasons changed in the former capital. A permanent mist settled and soaked summer till its deep colors ran like cheap dyes, leaving days of metallic grays and a rust like dried blood. The rain pounded the tiles.

One morning the concierge came into the dining-room evil-tempered because of an increase in the price of butter. She shouted into the hearing aid that twined from Herr Nadler's ear. "If only you were young again, Herr Nadler. You're honorable. You tried to save your motherland from Big Money once before. You'd do something now!"

Herr Nadler looked confused and muttered, *"Selbstverständlich, Frau . . . Frau . . ."*

The concierge's words blasted Charles Allen out of his lethargy. Brushing breadcrumbs from his mouth, he groped for the envelope in his pocket. The concierge forgot Herr Nadler and watched the American tugging at his trousers.

A Duty

According to the letter, Charles Allen was an heir. He had inherited an estate consisting of several bank accounts with no more than spare change in them, and a business and retail outlet called Die Schöne Heimat. The value of the stock had not been assessed, and the store was closed. The letter warned Charles Allen of his duty. He must decide within six months, by the beginning of November, whether to claim the inheritance. The name of the deceased was buried in the middle of the text. It read, "Johannes Allerhand."

When Charles first read this, the name rang like chimes on a door blown open by the wind. No one came in. Later, he remembered that "Johannes Allerhand" referred to his father.

He recalled a pudgy, thick-featured, balding man standing proudly in front of a Studebaker. A few spoken sentences went with this image, every one about an antique store that the Nazis had burned down on a night called Crystal in the autumn of 1938. It seemed to Charles that his father had never spoken about anything else.

It had certainly seemed so to his mother, Irma Allen. Charles remembered her complaining that long before he was born she had done her best to change the subject. In 1939, she packed two suitcases and dragged her husband to the boat in Bremerhaven. She called him "Johannes" when he boarded, and "John" by the time they disembarked. From New York she scolded him across the country by Greyhound, finally picking a small town called Athens in Oregon to settle in because of the wonderful scenery.

But the acquisition of a five-room wooden bungalow, an American passport, an American-born son, and a job as a waiter at Joey's Barbecue could not reorient this Johannes-turned-John. His wife kept at it. She cajoled him into changing the family name from Allerhand to Allen, she had everyone baptized, and after a few Sundays at church, she began to believe what she practiced.

Straining to recollect, Charles could only find his father on the periphery of his most important childhood memories. On Charles's fourth birthday, John Allen said there was no toy train in all America to compare with the old German ones. For Christmas he wished for his shop back. When Charles fell down a flight of stairs at five, John Allen picked him up and comforted him by telling him again about the "accident" that had cost him his business.

One Sunday morning, while driving home from Mass, John Allen heard news on the car radio: the German government was reimbursing former citizens who had lost property during the Third Reich. John Allen stopped the Studebaker and said, "I'm going to walk. I can't drive when I'm excited."

He left the family in the back seat, ran home, and packed his old suitcase. He flew to Germany the next morning. He was supposed to be back in Athens for Charles's first day of school but he never even wrote.

His wife stood in for him at Joey's until the owner lost patience with her because she never smiled. Then she went to work as a live-in housekeeper for an order of nuns called Immaculate Conception, where speaking was forbidden. At school Charles heard the sound of voices as a strange noise. His English never lost its German accent.

Irma Allen died the day her son passed his driving test. She was buried in the convent cemetery while he missed the first game of the World Series. Charles studied accounting for two years and took over the management of the convent finances. No one ever asked him questions, no one ever suspected about his family history. When notification of his father's will arrived from Germany, the mailman asked if he could have the stamps.

Later, Charles ripped them off with part of the return address. He thought: Who cares—let someone else keep the inheritance.

But his annual vacation was due again. For the past two years he had declined the chance to take even a day off. This time the Mother Superior said, "You must take a break." Charles obeyed. He went to a travel agency and, since no other destination occurred to him, he booked himself a thirty-day trip to Berlin.

The Inheritance Remembered

By the time Charles Allen reached the twenty-eighth day of his vacation, he felt on easy terms with Berlin. He had sampled all the city's tourist attractions, and most of the sweet desserts offered at its better coffeehouses. His twenty-eighth morning in the *Pension* seemed no different from the twenty-seven preceding it, until the concierge started to fret about Herr Nadler's honor.

The elderly Herr Nadler was the concierge's comfort. In a changing world, there was something permanent about him. He had the muscle tone of a former warrior who works out on the parquet before breakfast, and, no matter the circumstances, his posture always stayed aligned along its ramrod. His appearance had a crispness and whiteness that the concierge wished for her tablecloths.

Charles's posture was poor and his love of honor underdeveloped. He even hated the word, because the omission of the aspirated H seemed a mutilation of the English by the French. He liked to think that German, at least, had reliable, emphatic syllables. The concierge's were slurred by outrage as she addressed

her guests about the price of butter and praised Nadler because
he had fought for his country instead of trying to cheat people.
She considered money as necessary but distasteful as feces.

Hearing her words, urgency possessed Charles Allen. He hurried out of the breakfast room, abandoning a perfectly good half-
pat of butter.

A Dutiful Visitor

Charles Allen was not a shopper. Antiques bored him and he
disliked all forms of shabbiness. He would have walked past the
store, had he not inherited it. The facade repelled him, soot covered the front window, rust had overgrown and twisted the
metal sign that read DIE SCHÖNE HEIMAT. A dim light shone at the
back, and the door stood slightly ajar. Charles went inside. A tall,
bulky man picked his way slowly toward him through a clutter
of antiques. As he advanced he called, "Esther! A customer!"
Charles had no time to correct him.

A small woman flashed up to him, a confusing image of reds
and blacks that made him turn away, even as she addressed him.
"Are you buying or selling? We're actually closed."

Charles faced the man, who shrugged his shoulders at the
attention. "She's the boss." He wore a tailored suit, and his
round face gleamed with a close shave. "I'm just old Baruch, the
assistant, I have nothing to say. Maybe we give him a chance,
Esther. He has something worth buying, you don't know."

Looking at the floor, Charles brought forth his official letter,
which rustled loudly as he unfolded it. "I've come about this,"
he said.

The woman did not even acknowledge the paper. She said,

"So it's Allerhand's son. Good son. Turning up to claim what is his. Rubbish son!" She snapped her fingers and pointed at the door. Her companion's head jerked to look in the direction she pointed.

Charles Allen slunk to the door, brushing a stack of books that began to tumble slowly. Then she shouted in a hoarse voice, "Spoiled American Jew!"

Charles Runs Away

As Charles Allen scrambled out to the street, his jacket caught on the door handle and a seam tore loudly. Everything about him seemed to be coming apart. He ran. He wasn't very fast. At the next corner, a hand yanked at his arm. "Why don't you wait a minute?" It was she, the woman called Esther. He could no longer avoid looking at her and saw that her black hair reached down to her waist, and that a red, crooked mouth dominated her pale face. He felt without really thinking that she must be too old to be pretty. A silver Star of David shone in her décolletage.

"Oh, don't get carried away by a little unfriendliness. Who isn't spoiled nowadays? The war's over. It kept people in line. I'm spoiled too. A spoiled German Jewess. So now we're even. And I happen to be a beast, to top it off. Because I was treated like a beast. So don't blame me. Look, I did everything for Allerhand. For over fifteen years. I *made* Allerhand and when he dies, his son shows up with his palms held out. That's my reward. We're not talking about an ordinary sort of business here. It's complicated—and it's the only kind of work someone like me can do in Germany."

"You're right," yipped Charles on the street corner. "You keep the shop, it's only fair. Fair play, it's an American ideal I believe in." His hand drew up to his heart. "It wasn't my idea to come here, I'll go back to Oregon tomorrow. Excuse me for bothering you. Really, I didn't know. I'm going—"

The apologies disarmed her. "You're not like your father, are you?"

She wasn't like his mother.

He had never spoken to a woman who put color on her face. He couldn't decipher what it did to her beyond obscuring her features. He noted that the redness of her lips accentuated the whiteness of her teeth, but the color was smeared in one corner by a large scar. Her figure was sturdy. No, she was not Charles Allen's type, although he had no experience with women at all, and by thirty-five years of age he had long given up the expectation that he ever would. But he had his principles: he preferred blonds.

"I'm a businesswoman," she resumed, "so let's talk *tachles.*" She spoke the Yiddish word without effort. "You want something—everyone wants something! And I want something too. That's honest."

She moved closer to him. "And I don't want you to turn down your inheritance, even if it seems the easiest way for you. I want you to accept it, and let me continue to manage the shop, as I've always done. Otherwise, Die Schöne Heimat goes to the government. You can't possibly want to give your inheritance to the German state, that would be too grotesque."

"I'll give it to you," he said, trying to back away.

"Well, that sounds better." Suddenly she smiled at him. "Don't you want to see your father?"

Charles Goes to See His Father

"You can call me Frau Becker."

"I'm Mr. Allen."

"You're lying. Your name's Mr. Allerhand."

"Allen. Charles Allen. Changed name, maybe. But I never had another. You're Esther, aren't you? Esther Becker."

"You can call me Esther if you want. You have no sense of privacy in the land of the free, anyway. I'm sure you've never seen anything like my car, even in America, Charles."

Charles Allen had never paid attention to cars before; now he made an effort. The black Mercedes had a telephone, a bar, and leather bucket seats. "Eighty thousand," she said. She drove clumsily, both hands on the steering wheel, accelerating with little jerks. Charles watched the Star of David swing around her bosom. "What are you looking at?" she protested, her hand flying up to her neck, pulling her jacket closed. "It's cowardly to inspect someone like that. Like a border policeman. Inspect yourself first."

And at the next traffic light she looked him over with a quick glance, as if it sufficed to take in his short black hair, his rather handsome face, the neat dreary suit he always wore, the undemonstrative tie and thin leather belt, the shiny loafers on his flat feet. "There are two kinds of Jews in the world," she concluded. "The aggressive kind like me, and the passive, intelligent ones, just waiting for a beating. Like you.

"Your father was the only mixture of the two kinds I have ever known. He didn't look like a bully, but he was a bully, a sentimental bully. He used to cry about the human race, about Germany—the Schwarzwald! The Rhine!—Actually, the only thing that really moved him was his own feelings. Are you listening?"

"Yes."

"When he came here, he was just one of a lot of fellows with big noses turning up to claim reparations money. He wasn't very sensible about it, though, the way the others were. He spent every penny to buy back the store he had owned before the war. He tried to sell souvenirs there—bottles of Berlin air, toy bears, antiques. Listening?"

"Yes."

"The population was dispirited and starving, only the foreign soldiers had any money. Then he had some luck. He stumbled on other things to buy and sell. As an American, he could travel back and forth between the zones. He became a specialist in Nazi loot. Isn't that ironic? No one asked him any questions, he was allowed to possess valuables when nobody else could.

"The Germans never hated the Jews more than after the war, when it seemed the Chosen People had inherited the earth— moral superiority and money. Allerhand made a fortune, and was still unhappy. He began to feel guilty about being rich, he felt he had to do something for the money he earned. When the Wall went up he made that his business. So he became less rich, and by the time we met he was struggling again."

They drove away from the city center, west, until Esther stopped the car at the edge of a forest of very old tall trees. A metal fence staked a clearing in the woods. After they passed through a plain entrance gate, Charles saw the gravestones, gray welts on the forest floor. The starlings blew in black clouds through the trees.

Johannes Allerhand's grave was marked by a wooden plaque.

His son stood over it and felt the cold seep down into his shoes. He sidled closer to Esther and then another sensation assaulted him: an awareness of her smallness and roundness and warmness, of her woman's voice and the softness of her hair. At first only his body had this awareness, it simply bypassed his intelligence. When his mind became privy to the sensation, he lost the last of his already modest ability to make small talk.

"You know what? Here lies one who was a bad father to many," she said, speaking with such gayness that Charles wondered whether she was not rather indifferent to death. He was glad to disapprove of her a little. "He looked after me when I was younger. And when he was older I looked after him. It wasn't easy. He was very moody. If he was angry, he wouldn't talk, and his silence could last weeks and then months and was a dreadful punishment. Over the years he became more and more like the old Jewish God: humorless, all-knowing, and cruel. I couldn't imagine him sick. He never was. I never saw him injured. I used to joke that he had no blood at all.

"He never spoke about you, ever. I found out he had a son when he died. On the store documents you were listed as an owner. He must have had you in mind thirty years ago when he first came back to Germany. But after that—cancel any illusions if you have them—he forgot about you."

Inside Esther, a Mysterious Landscape

By the time Allerhand was buried, she appeared to have forgotten that he had died. She hardly enjoyed herself at his funeral—the rabbi was expensive, he was charging them his enemy tariff, and he performed listlessly. The five friends of the deceased in attendance were more appalled by his death than saddened by it, although they cried a fair amount and prayed loudly with the rabbi. The weather was just right, though: the ground was no longer frozen, so that Esther didn't worry about the grave diggers having trouble digging a hole, yet it wasn't so lovely as to make death seem poignant. Winter had definitely come to an end, the sky was clear and windy, and the crocuses were burrowing slowly through the soil. Esther had never felt sentimental about nature, but she recognized a pretty day; Allerhand must be enjoying it, wherever he was.

The party after the burial was enjoyable. Quite a number of people who had made themselves a nuisance to Allerhand during his lifetime showed up at Esther's apartment to sit around drinking beer, eating pretzels and cake, and telling fond jokes about the deceased, until they laughed or cried. Esther's tears ran black with mascara, as if some of the cemetery soil was lodged in her eyes. Her weeping was sporadic. Just as she was cackling at a remark whispered by the baby-faced Baruch, or launching into an anecdote or a mouthful of cake, black tears began to cascade down her face. The whites of her eyes gradually turned pink and then red, and she kept wiping the moisture off her face and protesting, "Dammit, *why* am I crying?"

When the doorbell rang, the guests stopped moving. Someone turned off the dance music on the radio. Esther suspected it could be Allerhand returning, the whole thing a stupid joke, but still she found the courage to open the door. She giggled at the sight: Frau Bilka, the landlady, fat enough to fill the doorway, holding red roses against the black dress she had put on for the occasion. "I want to pay my respects," the visitor said, as if the old-fashioned phrase was itself an important ingredient of consolation.

"We don't need your respects, Frau Bilka," Esther told her. "Really we don't. We'd prefer you kept your dog from making such a lot of noise in the morning when he attends to his bowels. And next winter, shoveling the snow from the front walk a bit more punctually, before it's frozen solid. That would be a way to pay your respects. But thank you for coming, and have a pleasant day, just the way I'm having." She closed the door again. Inside, she quoted herself to everybody. "That woman hated Johannes. Why should I be charitable?" Then she gave a booming laugh, which was a signal for the party to resume.

Nothing interrupted the festivities again, certainly not any talk about Allerhand's death. No one said as much as, Why did he do it! He had everything going for him in his old age. And in such a vile manner, so that his closest friends had their stomachs turn at the thought!

The Jewess Explains the Jews

They left the cemetery in the dark. On the brightly lit Kurfürstendamm Charles said he would return to his hotel, but she stopped him. "You won't. We have to talk. I'm inviting you." And she clamped her small hand around his arm and steered him to one of those vast coffeehouses where the elderly indulge their need for rococo. The ceiling was glutted with chandeliers and slowly drifting smoke, while down below the old women sat bent over coffees and *Torte*, their gray heads neat as tombstones.

Charles ordered *Apfelstrudel* with vanilla sauce and devoted himself to the pastry like a monk to prayer. He did not listen to Esther who, after settling her coat on the back of the chair and her mind on the least expensive cake on the menu, began a monologue about the virtues of saving money. She was far gone when she noticed her escort's inattentiveness. "Baruch says I am a financial genius," she exclaimed.

"Yes."

"But it is just a question of energy. And instinct. You have to know what to buy when. And whether a risk is worth taking. Last month, after Johannes died, I bought thirty thousand pairs of shoes from Bangkok; that was a comfort to me. They cost only 1.85 marks a pair. It took our women two weeks to scratch the Thai labels off, and then we sold them to a wholesaler for 4.85 a pair. That netted us 90,000 marks. Now they retail at 29.95 a pair, a price no customer can resist. Of course, I'll have a load of taxes to pay. You know?"

"Yes."

"You eat cake just like one of these old biddies," she laughed angrily. Then he pushed aside his plate in shame.

She consulted the check. "Eight marks for our measly cake and coffee. This waitress doesn't deserve a tip at all, but I'll round it up for her. No, I'll leave her twenty pfennig. No, twenty-five, that's a round sum, isn't it, 8.75." She rummaged through her purse. Charles handed her change.

"That'll do, although she doesn't deserve it," Esther said. "These coffeehouses make me so nervous with all those old Nazis sitting around enjoying themselves."

The waitress approached the table, but Esther waved her away. "Let me finish what I was saying, without anyone interrupting us. Listen to me, Charles," she demanded, "pretend you're a man."

He tried; he made an effort to appear interested, his face set in a mask he remembered seeing on a dark, handsome leading man in the movies when he was listening to a blond angel talk about her last tennis match at Southampton. But then he thought with irritation that Esther was not blonde and she was much too old for the interest of a leading man, and with an ugly scar. Yet she impressed him.

The waitress was not impressed. She loomed over their table. There were other customers waiting for places. She had taut yellow curls, and a sarcastic expression. Esther said very loudly, "These Aryans are simply not able to imagine the suffering of a Jewess in Germany."

The waitress turned away and busied herself with the neighboring table. "It's still an original sin to be Jewish here, and no baptism will clean it off you," Esther's voice pursued her.

"My parents had friends who hid them in Berlin until 1943. My father had nothing better to do in the attic of an office building than to impregnate his wife. Then he was terrified of the consequences, and sent her away wrapped in a rug in the back of a diplomat's car. She landed in Alsatia, where she had contacts. They hid her in a farmer's barn. They visited her at night. The farmer didn't know.

"When her contacts didn't come anymore, she slipped out and scavenged. She loathed the baby growing in her stomach. She dreaded my birth because she thought I would alert the farmer that she was hiding in his barn. She's hated me ever since."

The waitress stared at them from a distance.

"That's wonderful," Charles said.

"What's wonderful?" she said.

He shook his head. "Excuse me, I mean, you're so honest. About such a thing. It amazes me."

"Then take me home now."

Too Early to Go to Bed

He told himself there could be no harm in bringing her home. They didn't talk as they walked and his thoughts fluttered like birds competing for a roost: the Dodgers won against the Orioles today; there's no harm in walking; it must be terribly late, time for bed; the streetlights turn her black hair silver and her pale face black; with her messy mouth.

They had reached her apartment.

"Come up," she said.

"I shouldn't. The hotel closes at midnight."

"Then there's lots of time." She fumbled with the keys. "A *Pension,* not a hotel then. You must be on a very cheap trip."

"No, I'm not. It cost $749 all inclusive. That's a lot. Even a trip to Las Vegas, for instance, is cheaper, with the best hotel accommodations."

They reached a door, with a bronze plaque reading BECKER.

"You're like me, remembering a number like $749. I like that. Welcome to Esther's place," she said, flinging the door open.

"What a place!" he admitted. Vegetation filled it, growing from the high ceiling downward along special shelves to the floor. Nor were these common-cut flowers, like roses, tulips, or daisies. The gardener was discriminating: honeysuckle and grapevines twisted along a trellis heavy with fruit. Fuchsia grew in rows and amaryllis in big pots. In one corner fanned a lilac shrub. A table stood beneath the grapevine, with four chairs around it. The carpet beneath was lawn. "Plastic," said Esther, "is my passion.

"Ghastly, isn't it? We Jews have no taste. I read an article once on why. It comes from generations always having to move on. We don't form attachments to furniture. It's too combustible. I keep only the necessities. Jewelry, coins, that's what we like. And plastic flowers you don't have to water." She led him down a long hall to an immaculate kitchen. "This is where your father died.

"He never ate until I told him to. One day I said, "Hans, come home with me, you must eat an egg with *Bratkartoffeln.*" He sat down at the kitchen table, and I set his place, with fork, knife, a plate, his glass. I put down salt and pepper. Then I fried him an egg, with my back turned toward him. I was just thinking: Maybe he doesn't have to have *Bratkartoffeln,* toast will do, it's cheaper, when I turned around. And he was lying with his face on the plate."

She smiled politely. The scar on her upper lip stretched. "What's that scar," Charles asked, "on your mouth?"

"I was twenty when I met him. He was like a father to me, but a possessive father—no man was good enough for me. So in a way, he had the best fifteen years of my life for himself. Then he disappeared.

"I'm annoyed, that's all. Sad, no, why should I be sad? I'm a survivor. Who do I have here? A few friends, like Baruch. A mother who has hated me since before I was born.

"My mother is half-dead now. I have a half-dead mother in a

home for the half-dead. I used to visit her on Saturdays, although those visits were the most arduous work I did all week.
On the Sabbath, good Jewish children visit their parents and
hope they die soon. It's an old tradition. And my mother is de-
ranged. Her memory is a black hole that sucks in everything. The
one thing it spits out again is how much I owe her, as a daughter.
For hiding me in her stomach. For bearing me at all. I should be
grateful to her bodily functions."

Then she resumed her tour. "This is my bedroom. You can
look at it, why not?"

Her Bedroom

Her bedroom had a bed.

To the male virgin, a woman's bed is a monument of overwhelming grandeur. His heart thrashes. He is terrified of using
his nose and smelling scents strange and wrenching beyond
imagination, so he pants through his mouth. Glimpse of a wardrobe. Then his vision is snared in the mound of pillows and the
rumpled sheets.

"Let me show you the extra room," Esther said calmly.

The Extra Room

"Why don't you just sleep here tonight?"

He made no reply.

"It's easier than going back to that cheap *Pension*. I usually
have a roomer. I'm just looking for a new one now. It's actually

a maid's room. I make a small profit for the trouble and risk I go to; they can use the kitchen, and the hall toilet, not the bathroom. And it's furnished. Not with my things. With your father's."

Furnished meant jammed with gleaming ebony pieces, it meant the limitation, or rather the elimination, of any human movement beyond walking three steps, opening a wardrobe, sitting down at a dressing-table with three mirrors that tripled the furniture, or lying down on the medieval bed. One wall was taken up with a silhouette. A black woman knelt down, her head thrown back, her long hair pulled by the devil. In his other hand the devil brandished a whip.

"Your father claimed I posed for that," Esther said. Then she blew him a kiss and left him.

He could hear her next door running the water in the bath. Charles relaxed, took off his shoes, and sat upright on the bed. The water gurgled in the bathroom, a glass rattled, the cabinet opened and closed. He leaned cautiously against the headboard and fell asleep.

Charles Needs Good Luck

In Berlin, dawn is greeted by the concierges entering their courtyards and crowing, "There's to do! There's to do! There's always to do!" Those who cannot sleep on must endure the racket of *Tüchtigkeit*—efficiency—a dreadful noise in any profession, but the concierge has the most powerful instruments at her disposal: the garbage bin and the hose, the broom and the hacking cough.

Charles Allen woke up with impressions of Esther in his ears, in his nose, on his arms. He stood up, checked his three reflections in the mirror. The left side showed his prominent nose with curved nostrils; the middle reflected a man who felt embarrassed by his mouth and black-lashed eyes, as if their large size was a demand for attention he really did not seek; and the right side was filled out by an illkempt sort in a wrinkled suit.

He ran his fingers through his hair and smoothed his suit. Then he gave a friendly nod to the girl being flogged, and sought out the kitchen.

"Ready for breakfast?" called a motherly voice. "I'm going to make you an egg."

She was warmhearted, she was interested in his well-being, she was womanly. The three W's that make a female, speculated Charles, driving his fork into the egg yolk.

"You can stay here with me for a few days while we sort out the business," she said, when he had finished. "You'll save. Let's go get your suitcase."

Charles agreed. "I can save 80 marks a day," he said, trying to share her interest in money. He enjoyed leaning back to make room for her to sponge off the table.

"You'll save 40 marks. It'll cost you 40 marks a night to stay at my place, with breakfast."

It was Saturday. Die Schöne Heimat was closed. After noon, everything would shut down until Monday. "It used to depress me that for forty-eight hours I couldn't go shopping or do any business," Esther said. "That was my Sunday Depression. Then I found out that lots of businesses stay open around the clock."

The day passed pleasurably. Esther doted on him. She allowed him to read his newspaper, fed him at regular intervals, tidied up around him, and, best, did not engage him in too much conversation.

In the evening she drove him to the Pension Central, where the concierge fussed about waiting up the previous night to let Herr Allen in, who hadn't come at all. She wondered why he was moving out two days early and demanded that he pay for them anyway.

Charles paid. As she double-checked the bills, the landlady became sentimental about Americans, remembering John Kennedy for his youthfulness and honesty. She fetched Herr Nadler and they stood at the door like an honor guard as Charles Allen trudged out with his suitcase. When he reached the bottom of the steps Charles turned back to look and Herr Nadler grunted, "Good luck to you."

Why should I need good luck? Charles wondered. He calculated that by staying with Esther he saved half the money he would pay for a hotel, so he could afford to stay twice as long. He told himself this was a reason to stay.

He was sitting up on the narrow bed reading the newspaper when Esther came in to say good-night to him. She sat down next to him and said, "We can sign a contract on Monday, you can leave here with happy memories." She placed her hand palm up on his knee. He cowered. She laughed, and stood up again.

Much later she made a lot of noise walking up and down the hall in front of his door, her footsteps a drumroll of suspense.

Charles Suffers

On Monday, after a long, idyllic weekend, Charles faced the mirrors in his room and reflected about his future. He saw himself explaining his odd state of mind to the Mother Superior. "The decision about the inheritance has proven complicated," he spoke boldly. He imagined the Mother Superior laughing happily and then breaking into the song "Climb Every Mountain."

He watched his face turn red with shame. He knew he was much too cowardly to confide in her. But confide what, for heaven's sake? he asked himself. The word twisted around in his mouth: flesh.

Every minute that Charles was near Esther, taboos were crunching in his psyche. He had already broken the biggest taboo of all—he had felt curiosity. Now he wanted to satisfy this curiosity by studying her. In this way he expected to enjoy her. It never crossed his mind that, in order to do this, he might have to leave the vantage point of a Catholic virgin.

But that morning he caught only a glimpse of her as she sped by him on her way to the bathroom. He posted himself outside and listened. She emerged after a long time, dressed in a black suit, her hair a black mass over her carefully decorated, girlish face. She practically knocked him over coming out, and then snapped at him. "What are you hanging around here for? I can't bear anyone seeing me asleep, or just gotten up, I hate pasty, swollen, sleepy faces. Stop staring at me, please."

Later she came and told him to take a bath. "You may as well look good for your last morning in Berlin." Those moments in the sanctum of her bathroom, surrounded by a vast array of her cosmetics, proved the happiest of his day.

By the time she knocked for him to hurry, she had orchestrated breakfast. He absorbed the image of her standing at the old stove in the yellow light of the kitchen. He noted exactly how she opened the oven with the pot holder, how she had to hop backward, and then blink, grabbing a napkin to check her mascara, before removing the rolls and spreading them with butter. "Have some honey, it's good for your potency," she said.

She seemed to like his passivity, the greed with which he ate her buttered rolls. She obviously drew out the moment when she slid the spoon into the honey, rolled it to keep the syrup from dripping. As she slipped it into his mouth she said, "This breakfast is the long and short of a pleasant relationship. I'm kind of sorry you're leaving."

He swallowed and told her, "I think I'll stay and think about the store for a few more days. There's no hurry. I have till the ninth of November to decide." He licked the honey from his lips, and she startled him by clattering the sticky spoon on the table.

"Oh sure, fine," she said. "I guess you're not going to be so generous with the store after all. Take it, you said. Because you were scared of me. Then, when I'm nice to you, you want to keep it. Sure, fine, you can stay with me if you like. Till the ninth. But then you'll be just a roomer here, do you understand? Nothing fancier. Not a friend, not a sunny boy I have to mother. Pay rent and you can stay. But you can make up your mind about the shop without me. I'm going now. You can wait here for me."

He followed her out of the kitchen and watched her hurtle around the apartment. She locked the door to her room, to the kitchen, even to the bathroom, pointing out the guest toilet he could use. She didn't want him near her personal things, she said, enunciating the word "personal" so that it left a puncture wound in his ambitions. He accompanied her to the threshold and watched despondently her high-heeled boot click on the first step, then her slow disappearance down the staircase, marked by a shortened torso and finally only the parting in the middle of her head.

He waited for her to return. He waited at home, and then he waited at a coffee shop. He drizzled the sugar on the table to spell WWW, the three W's that make a woman. When the waitress approached he brushed it hastily on the floor. Back in Esther's apartment, he sat on his bed reading the *Tribune*'s baseball scores and suddenly his lips formed the word, "W-w-w-ait," and then bitterly, "good luck." In his head he heard himself shout: I can't wait! He could not understand why his waiting did not force her to come back.

He found he could no longer remember what she looked like. He drew up a list of her attributes:

ESTHER BECKER:

Hair Color:	Black, like billions of other people in the world.
Shape of Face:	Oval, far from perfect at the jowls and below the chin.
Color of Eyes:	Thick black paste on the lashes. The eyebrows absent, replaced by two sweeps of a pencil.
Mouth:	An abnormal mouth, the upper left corner is stained by a scar. She has a way of pursing her lips before smiling, and she has perfect, even, white teeth.
Hands:	Sparrow-sized, they flutter when she talks. She wears a ring on every finger, except the ring finger. Apparently her nails won't grow.

He wrote, *"Torso:"* and left it blank, continuing with:

     Feet: Size thirty-five, my age!

He read through his work, realized he didn't know what color eyes she had, hated himself for being so sloppy in his research, and turned on the television.

Late at night Charles left 40 marks on the plastic coffee table in the living room and tried to sleep. Much later he became aware of her return. He listened as she paced down the hall, he heard exactly and with interest how she used the toilet, turned off lights on her way to her bedroom, and snapped her door shut. Then he fell asleep. Charles awoke with the relief that follows an illness. He laughed as someone banged garbage-bin lids in a rooster rage, and said to himself, "There's so much to do today!" He pulled back the curtains, saw the blue sky and, exultant, went to find Esther. But she had already left the apartment.

Charles Allen's suffering had reached saturation point. Suddenly, he rebelled. She could not forbid him to look for her.

Charles Finds What He Wants

Finding Esther wasn't hard. Die Schöne Heimat was located just a few blocks away. There, in person, was the object of his search, bending over, so that all he saw through the glass door was her boots and her backside.

He began to address her as he stepped over the threshold. "I'd like to see the store records, that's why I've come. I'm an accountant. I'll just look through them and bother no one,'' all the time grinning with delight.

Charles Learns About Business

''What really brings you to your store?'' asked Baruch. He polished a heavy silver menorah. ''Your father's last acquisition, not many buyers for a seven-branch menorah from Alsatia, even though it's very rare, nineteenth century. I'm going to offer it to Father Renard as a special holder for votive candles; the real money's in Christian articles—diamond rosaries, antique crucifixes, thuribles, pyx, and relics. Renard takes everything. We pick up a lot from Italy, where they don't lock the churches.'' He held up the menorah. ''The shop thrives on . . .''

''The shop thrives on candles and furniture,'' Esther interrupted. ''We buy and sell.'' She unlocked a cabinet and brought out dusty ledgers. ''We introduced East German candles to West Berlin. We get them from a firm in Dresden, we call them Holy Land candles. Most candles come from the old 'family firms' in Fulda. They grew big making candles for Hitler's army chaplains to burn at field masses.''

Baruch reproached her. ''So dry, Esther. You've got to make it colorful for him, so he'll enjoy himself. There's nothing wrong with the candles made in Fulda except that they're too fancy, nothing looks like a candle any more. Your father had this idea to import plain white cheap candles from the Communist countries. If you want to know the truth,'' he put the menorah down with a sigh, ''Johannes Allerhand had no sense of humor, and was always worrying about aesthetics.''

''It wasn't a question of humor or aesthetics at all,'' corrected

Esther. She piled the ledgers on a table. "He thought he was contributing to détente. Here, Charles, you wanted something to do. Have a good time."

Baruch put the menorah down and tapped a forefinger on the table. "This, for example, is a typical sample of what Esther calls 'Buy and Sell.' A Galé table, legally acquired yesterday from a stupid woman. I saw an ad in the papers, 'An old table with a picture of a river carved into the top.' The woman wanted one hundred marks for it; I got her down to seventy-five. It'll sell for five thousand."

"He's interested in the books, Baruch, not in your stories."

They left Charles alone with the stack of ledgers. He heard them quarreling in the back room about Baruch's garrulousness.

The first store records, dated 1956, showed that Johannes Allerhand had paid for the store with a lump sum.

Apparently 1956 was a bad year as the store just broke even; 1957 was just as bad.

The year 1958 was bad too. The economic boom of the sixties bypassed Die Schöne Heimat. The store's failure was neatly recorded. "This business made no money!" Charles marveled.

"We do it for pleasure." Esther came into the room, took the ledgers and returned them to the cabinet. "There are other sources of income," she added. "Are you absolutely sure you're Allerhand's son?"

Inside Esther, a Mysterious Landscape

Johannes Allerhand followed Esther up the four flights of stairs, falling farther and farther behind her. She hated the fact that she could walk so much faster than he. "Hurry up, will you?" she called down at each landing. She could see part of his slowly moving shoulder and fedora. He panted. He was too fat and he was too old. When he reached the apartment door, she had slammed it shut, and he had to ring the bell. She took a long time coming to open the door again. "I've already started lunch," she said. "Although you shouldn't eat anything." She let him in and smiled grudgingly.

"You let me decide that myself," he replied. He was still strong as an ox emotionally: he didn't care enough about her to mind her contempt. "I wouldn't mind having some *Bratkartoffeln.*" He looked at her maliciously. "You be a nice girl and make me some *Bratkartoffeln.* With bacon."

She had no bacon. "You're old and horrible," she replied. "One oughtn't allow you to eat. Starve you to death, for humanitarian reasons."

He began to laugh and then he stopped laughing and said, "No. You depress me. I'm beginning to regret things."

"Don't ask me to count up all the things I regret," she replied, now only reluctantly continuing the squabble. She unbuttoned his coat for him. She had already set the kitchen table for two, and when she turned away from him, he was sitting at his place, holding his knife and fork expectantly; the eagerness for food always touched her. But she was not going to make him his potatoes. She made fried eggs; they sizzled and the pan banged.

She turned around, holding the pan, to slide the eggs onto his plate, and then she saw what he had done: he had put the knife way back into his mouth, propped the end on the table, and let his head fall down on it. It held him upright, but as she watched, his head rolled over onto the plate.

"You filthy despicable pig, how I hate you," she told him.

Esther Begins to Educate Charles

"What's missing in Charles is common sense," said Baruch. "It's all blah blah inside his brain. Maybe you should clarify the situation for him here."

"Clarify?" asked Esther.

"Talk to him. Go for a walk."

"He's too badly dressed. I don't want to be seen with him."

Esther and Baruch stood over Charles and pulled him up from his chair. "You're much too thin," Esther said. "You'll need a warmer coat. You can have one of these here. I bought two hundred of them."

Charles stood up straight. The coat was black mink. "Now you need a hat," she said. "I've got a nice gray fedora lying around somewhere."

Later he regretted that he had refused the hat. Esther spoke about nothing else but how handsome hats looked on men, fedoras in particular, she had a weakness for them, she could not bear a man without a hat, and then to say no to such a fine model, she could not forgive him. They went out for a walk anyway, because she said he had to learn a bit about his father. He thought she was still trying to prove a point about the hat when she took him to an open space where nothing prevented the wind from rushing into his ears. Two cranes were heaping the sand and rubble into dunes. One side of the area was marked by that gray, ordinary barrier covered with gay graffiti that arouses such emotions in the tourist's heart—the Berlin Wall. The tourists all wear hats, Esther pointed out. She wound her red scarf around her ears. She always wore the wool scarf, she admitted, even in a summer heat. It was a talisman.

"It was the only thing my mother saved from her trip to Alsatia. She wore it when she was hiding in the barn. She had it on when I was born. I found it in her closet a few years ago. She didn't want to give it to me, but who valued my birth more, her or me? Anyway, I need to be indulged."

The wind buffeted the two cranes, but the whirring of the machinery remained constant and so rather soothing. Finally, she changed the subject. "They're smoothing out bad ground. Here lies the Gestapo building," she said, "where Eichmann pushed his little pen."

He was embarrassed. She wanted to see his reaction to something that jarred him. He tried to cover up. "So what?" he said. He blushed and argued, "The wall is much more interesting. The graffiti are surely the most entertaining anywhere! Look at that one: 'Berlin is the asshole of the world.' " He realized as he chattered that he must appear foolish. "And this: 'high jumping forbidden.' "

She watched him. He giggled and his body swayed, bowed by the wind of his shame. He went on, " 'Humpty Dumpty Was Here,' well, I guess I am like Humpty, no one will ever be able to put me together again."

Suddenly the motors of the cranes were silenced. The day turned as quiet as it was gray, and the lights of the watchtowers on the other side of the wall went on. He shivered, seeing that she was watching him. In panic, he turned toward her and slapped his arm awkwardly around her shoulder; when she did not withdraw, he placed the other arm around her and tightened the embrace.

The Embrace

Heat rose from the opening of Esther's coat and bathed Charles's face. He trembled, and steadied himself on her shoulders. His face sank into the long hair that enveloped her neck and the rough red scarf, where he smelled a scent he knew to be perfume. He did not disintegrate. He became aware of his palms sliding along soft material and of his body pressing into a warm, yielding surface. He did not burn up or melt down, he was merely indecisive and, to his astonishment and relief, a bit bored. And she? She accepted the gesture, she neither warmed to it nor repelled it. She stood absolutely still. After a moment, he recalled his arms one after the other, soldiers who had gone out on a mission without orders, smiled at her and said, "I'm sorry."

Esther's Lesson

Released, she did not reply but rummaged around in her handbag until she found a small jewelry case. Inside the case was a tattered newspaper clipping. She said, "This place is special to me. This is where I was born again." She handed the clipping to Charles.

It showed a young woman crawling out of a hole beneath the old red-brick wall. The scene had been shot at night: outside the spotlight created by the photographers' blitz, everything was swampy. In the foreground, a bulky male figure in a fedora, with his back turned to the photographer, extended his hand to help the young woman out of the last millimeters of her confinement. The girl was looking up at her savior. The girl was Esther.

"Who is that?" asked Charles, pointing to the man.
"Your father."

Charles Is Unsettled

Charles did not wish to continue the walk. He did not want to
see the new museum, or the kinky café on Stresemann Strasse,
or attend a party at a rich man's house. He did not want to talk,
he did not want to listen, he did not want to know anything
about Esther, Berlin, or his father.

Charles wanted to go home.

"And where is home?"

"Drop me off at the store, please. I want to have another look
at those books before I go back to America."

"The books will tell you nothing. Accountants aren't God, you
know. And we are missing a party."

At the store he picked out the volumes 1963 to 1967, which
corresponded to the years when the wall was built from red
brick. Charles knew from the guided tours that tunnel escapes
were impossible after the East Germans replaced the brick with
gray cement. Quite a number of people had been put out of
work, including, perhaps, his father. From the books he learned
that in 1965 Johannes Allerhand had taken a manager onto his
payroll named Esther Becker. He paid her a sum of 6,000 marks
per annum, "plus commissions." The commissions were not
noted.

The merchandise seemed to correspond to Baruch's descrip-
tion—religious candles bought from a firm in Israel that organized exports from the East Bloc and sold them at a profit to

West German churches. There were no unusual expenditures at all until 1967, when Allerhand bought an office supply shop and then sold it again two weeks later at a loss.

"Can you explain this purchase of an entire office supply store, please?"

"We needed office equipment," Esther told him, "without having to show a receipt for it. So we bought a full store and sold an empty one."

"It's a secret to buy office equipment?"

"D'you realize we're missing a good party because of your nonsense?" she said.

He ignored her. She watched him as he quietly, patiently, went through the store records. Seeing him in that pose, Esther suffered an unpleasant memory. It enclosed her, like a locked room.

Inside Esther, a Mysterious Landscape

There comes a moment in a relationship between two people when the power leaves one of them and alights on the other. So it happened with Allerhand and the woman he employed as his manager and assistant. One minute she was unpacking an antique tea set in the back room, and he was berating her after he heard a cup jingling. She should take more care. It was a dull, hot Sunday night in August. She was cool in a cotton dress, her hair in a long braid down her back, while the heat erupted under his expensive starched shirt. They were interrupted by a knock on the back door.

Allerhand grumbled. He did not want to be bothered. "Put

that box away, will you," he told Esther. Then he unlocked the door.

There stood humble Herr Feigl, malformed Herr Rosen, and voluble but unintelligible Herr Rother. His colleagues. They sidled into the room in soft shoes and pastel linen suits, they peered around, cleared their throats, did not smile once, and passed on a message, one after the other, first with Herr Feigl's raspy voice, then with the Yiddish accent of Herr Rosen, and finally with the rapid, mispronounced syllables of the Polish Herr Rother: the Herr Direktor did not like what Allerhand was doing with his business practices. The Herr Director felt Herr Allerhand was giving the Jews a bad name. Die Schöne Heimat Company should switch businesses, go into something lucrative but legal, like furs or diamonds. Candles and antiques were a paltry front for this wicked, politically explosive commerce.

Of course Allerhand should have thrown them out. Instead he tried to defend himself. He said he was doing Jews a service, maybe not the Jews who ran jewelry shops or imported furs companies, but the other Jews, the ones stranded in the East who still needed help. Then Allerhand became sad. What an irony it was, how repellent and trivial. Tears welled up in his deep-set black eyes, he walked straight up to them and he said, "Please leave me alone now to my disappointment." But he failed. Instead of leaving, they smirked and said, "From a converted Jew we have to take such shenanigans? No!"

Then Allerhand's self-righteousness failed him. He jerked around to Esther. And in turning to her he surrendered his supremacy in their relationship. At once, she took over.

"That'll be all now," she clipped. "I've suffered enough for my Jewishness not to be pestered by some frustrated businessboys who happen to belong to my faith." And she pushed them along as though they were schoolchildren until she could close the door behind them.

Johannes Allerhand sat in his store crying, crying for the loss of his dignity. Esther stood at the door, her back turned toward him, and listened to his sobs as if they were chamber music.

Esther Explains

"Office equipment is useful for forging papers. Not only title deeds, receipts, sales records, and warranties of authenticity, but also visas and travel documents, for those who need them. Now can we go to the party? I want to see my friends."

Charles hated friends. But Esther obviously liked them. The party host was definitely a friend: he whispered, "Don't disgrace me, darling," to Esther as they entered his heavyset villa.

Henry Rosen was celebrating his son's bar mitzvah with the other Rosens from Tel Aviv, Caracas, Cincinnati, and Johannesburg. In his son's honor, he had also invited all of his business colleagues, who included almost all the Christians he knew.

"Disgrace you? If you don't want me to disgrace you, then you shouldn't have invited me," Esther told the host. "But you do want me to disgrace you."

They went to the cloakroom and added their coats to a mass of fur. Charles hadn't seen Esther change her clothes. She wore what he at first took to be a rabbit costume, a white dress with black patches, a paw pattern at the cuff, and a puff like a bunny tail at the back. Rosen evidently expected something unusual. He followed Esther into the cloakroom, waited until she removed her coat and then sighed with relief. "Nice, Esther, a real evening dress."

She turned on him. "Don't criticize."

"Did I criticize?"

"People have to accept me the way I am or they're not worth bothering about anyway. Let's find Baruch," she said to Charles. "These people here aren't my friends at all." Rosen smiled and returned to his post at the entrance. The crowd parted for Esther, and it seemed to Charles that the other guests regarded her critically. It must be her odd dress, he thought, or her wild black hair, or her pulling *me* along by the hand.

"Here are my friends," she said, when they reached the farthest end of the room. Charles recognized Baruch's fat face on the other side of a coffee table. Esther marched him into the limelight. "Introducing Johannes's little son, Charles!"

"Hans's son?" voices asked.

"He had a son?"

"A convert!" Esther poked him down into a chair. She adjusted the bunny tail and squeezed in next to him. Her thighs shook when she talked. "Charles'll have to tell you about the conversion . . . Oh, it's dreadfully funny . . . I mustn't start to laugh . . . Tell it from the beginning, Charles, when the priest was so bored with babies and pepped up when he saw a flock of Jewish lambs . . ."

The group of faces regarded Charles Allen and he replied mechanically, "It was nothing. The altar boy said, 'Wow!' when he saw us, and the priest took him outside and I heard him scold, 'We do not say "Wow!" at a conversion.' "

"He's been ashamed of being Jewish ever since," Esther said. "I was caught lying about it once. I was playing the question game in the courtyard—you know it? You make a circle, and one child stands in the middle. Then everyone in the circle claps their hands and fires questions at the child in the center, who has to answer yes or no. Do you like the color red? Does your mother wear perfume? Clap, clap. The joke is to ask normal, banal questions and then suddenly you ask: 'Are you in love with so-and-so?', and the child in the middle goes to pieces denying it.''

"Why don't we play now?" someone said. "Henry's parties are always so boring."

Someone else agreed. "I love games about lying!"

A consensus was reached: the company wanted Baruch in the middle.

Baruch resisted. "Inge won't like it, will you?"

A chubby, sultry, middle-aged woman at his side replied, "Inge will love it!"

"Baruch in the middle! I'll finish my story later," said Esther. Charles felt her weight shift against him, as she whispered, "Inge's Protestant!"

Baruch lowered himself onto the glass coffee table. "You better answer honestly," warned Inge, and set a rapid rhythm.

The others leaned forward in their chairs, eager for spectacle. Two identical twins from the Soviet Union clapped madly out of turn. They hardly understood German, Esther told Charles. They had grown up in the Lithuanian provinces, inseparable in thought, word, and deed. At their fifth arrest for stealing lightbulbs and toilet paper from hotel bathrooms, a psychiatrist diagnosed kleptomania and Soviet officials asked them if they wouldn't like to emigrate to Israel. They missed their connecting flight to Tel Aviv in West Berlin, and stayed put. After their fifth arrest for stealing jewelry and cameras, the twins were brought to the attention of the Jewish community's welfare office. There they found a foothold in the person of Henry Rosen, who put them to work in his real estate business. They hadn't been in trouble since.

Clap, clap!

"Have you been to Vilna?" asked the first twin.

"No," said Baruch.

"Have you been to Riga?" asked the second.

"No imagination," answered Baruch.

"Is your real name Baruch?" called Esther.

"According to my mother, yes," replied the victim.

"Are the police looking for you?" asked Esther's neighbor, a young man named Leon.

"They've never looked for me!" asserted Baruch.

"Are you in love with Inge?" asked Inge.

"If necessary," said Baruch, heaving himself off the coffee table. "This game is for the poor liars among us and those without appetites. I heard the buffet is open. Excuse me."

The twins followed. "They follow him everywhere. He can't go to the toilet alone," Inge complained. "How about you, Leon, aren't you hungry?"

Leon was watching his biceps as he pumped his arm. "Without clapping my hands, I want to know what our convert is doing here among us. His profession. That sort of thing."

"I'm an accountant," said Charles Allen.

Inge cheered. "An accountant! How unusual. And you, Leon, what do you do?"

"I'm a crook," the vain young man replied.

This conversation went on until Baruch reappeared looking red and ruffled. "This is some celebration," he said. "Esther, you and your heir better hurry before that buffet disappears."

Charles was released from the pressure of Esther's thigh, only to be forced to eat in public, an act that turned his face red, not from exertion so much as shame: opening his mouth, salivating, chewing and swallowing wet-lipped, his Adam's apple bobbing and Leon and Esther watching him.

"How does this clapping game story end?" Leon asked, checking his reflection in the gaze of the women around him.

"Speech! Speech!" cried Henry Rosen.

"I'm going to tell you about how I came to Germany from Israel. By way of explaining my pride in this bar mitzvah. I came back to Germany not as a Jew but as an Israeli. In Israel I was in the air force as a fighter pilot. I was strong. I came here to look around and I liked what I saw. Germany is the land of opportunity, the freest country in Europe! So I decided to stay. As an Israeli guest, I was always careful to behave correctly here. I am a hundred and fifty percent correct! And, nevertheless, I've been very successful here, and I have made enough money to have such a big bar mitzvah. And I wanted an expensive party like this because you never know with money: here today, gone tomorrow. And at least my boy Lonny will always have this as a memory. I'm grateful to this country for giving me a chance to supply Lonny with this precious memory! Tonight, I want to take this opportunity to thank Germany!"

He twirled and waved at the corner, where a band of musicians waited to strike the first note of the German national anthem.

Then Henry Rosen made his way through the crowd, shaking hands, puffing up with all the compliments.

"Esther! Darling! Isn't this beautiful!" Rosen had reached them. "And you're beautiful. I should have married you, maybe. What a beauty. And now you have a new friend, who is he, he looks nice, a little young for you, introduce me."

"Charles, this is my old heartthrob Henry."

"You're right, that's exactly it, heartthrob. I feel it right now."

"If only you had nice teeth, Henry. I could never have a man with such bad teeth. Bad teeth, bad bones. I would never let you kiss me."

Henry Rosen looked dazed. "Nobody ever told me that before," he said, his forefinger tapping his brown front teeth. "Not one woman. Not even Wanda." He moved away, tears in his eyes. The orchestra played a moderate foxtrot.

"The end of your stupid story, Esther," persisted Leon.

"Leave her alone, Leon," said Baruch, dancing by with Inge.

"We're celebrating our own anniversary tonight," said Inge. "My fifth year as welfare recipient."

Baruch stepped back and she danced on without him. While she moved her legs she moved her mouth—she told them her history, how she had briefly held a job as a secretary, then hurt her back on a skiing holiday. As she couldn't work as a secretary any more she was waiting for the welfare office to provide her with an acceptable alternative. Baruch listened from the sidelines, his eyes passionate. When she finished, he grabbed her around the waist, hoisted her above his head and said, "After the nuclear holocaust, my Inge will survive with the rats."

Turkish waiters appeared with sugary kosher wine in champagne glasses. The band took a break and Esther's friends regrouped around the coffee table. This time Esther sat right down in Charles's lap, placed her arms around his neck, and laid her head on his shoulder. She closed her eyes. Charles could feel her breath against his neck. He peered around her, trying to ignore what was happening to him, and listened to Inge and Baruch arguing about whether they were in love. Esther stirred in his lap. "I'm used to you," Baruch argued, "nothing else. I'm used to the television programs you like to watch, and your fried potatoes."

"And I'm used to your conceit and your bad character," said Inge.

"Esther, wake up and finish the story!" Leon called from the other end of the table. "About being caught lying. I am famished for stories about exposed liars."

"No, please don't finish the story, I can't hear it one more time," pleaded Baruch.

Esther sat up in Charles's lap.

She finished her story. "Well, we played this clapping game constantly when I was a child. I adored it. But one day I was afraid to play because I was madly in love with a little boy named Fabian. So when I came in the middle I dreaded the question, 'Are you in love with Fabian?' But instead they asked, clap, clap, 'Are all your grandparents Aryan?'"

"And you started to cry," Baruch sneered.

Esther ignored him. "And I started to cry. My mother heard me from upstairs, she came running down and the children asked her, what was wrong, why was I crying, and she said, 'Oh, she's sensitive about everything, the poor girl.' She took me upstairs and everyone thought she was going to comfort me. Then she beat the shit out of me."

"Oh Esther," complained Baruch, "you and that boring story. Ten times ago, I prayed that God would spare me the torture of ever hearing it again. God lets me suffer. I was in Auschwitz, isn't that enough? I shouldn't have to listen to these stories! The Germans behave decently to the Jews now. What more do you want?" He cupped his belly with both huge hands. "Look at this.

Sauerbraten, Knödel, Torte, Bier. As for your mother: I've never even seen her. Does she exist? Is she a monster?"

Esther Leaves a Party

"Not that vase!"

"Watch the coat rack!"

"Such an embarrassment."

"Help with the coats, there are hundreds of coats . . ."

"Oh, what a disgrace."

A Seduction Attempt

"Blind, deaf and dumb. Now I understand what he sees in Inge. His type is responsible for all the trouble. Sometimes I hate Baruch enough to think he deserved his concentration camp. He would sell his own people for a penny, he's only interested in money, and completely insensitive. If that's not subhuman, what is?"

She sat on the curb, her feet in the street. Charles hovered around her, worrying what passersby would think, or worse, say. He said nothing to her and after a while she stood up and walked off. He watched her go, and then ran after her in panic.

She did not speak to him, but permitted him to walk beside her. Soon he felt her hand snaking into the crook of his arm. It was not dangerous, just a hand, not as bad as the thigh had been, yet it left an eerie feeling in his arm. He was delighted that she was not walking away without him, but at the same time he could barely control his desire to shake her off. They turned down her street and she pressed against him. When they reached her door he took advantage of the stairwell to pull out of her grasp, so that his viper arm lashed at her side.

He reached the guest room ahead of her. She followed him, shedding her coat on the way, coming toward him in her rabbit dress, cornering him next to the dressing-table. The mirror captured his mink coat, and her gradual approach. She was holding something. Then she helped him out of the coat, tossing it carelessly on the bed—in his despair he thought: At least the bed is now fully occupied with coats and no one can expect me to sit or lie down on it—and then she placed something on his head.

"Turn around, sit down, and look at yourself," she said.

He did as he was told and saw a swarthy young man in a blue suit with a white yarmulke on his head. Behind him a woman in white, a Star of David glittering at her bosom. Fascinated, he watched as her arms slid around his chest and her cheek came down to his. In the mirror he saw how she bent down to him, and how, driven by the image, he responded: a Jewish lover.

The image proved fleeting. No sooner did he turn his head than it was gone. Charles struggled briefly out of a kiss to seek his reflection again, but the yarmulke tumbled off his head, and he found only his familiar self in the mirror.

Esther slid down around his knees and buried her head in his lap. He felt terribly embarrassed. He shook her off by standing up, and apologized. "I'm sorry, I prefer blondes. I can't help it."

She stood up after him and said, "I prefer blonds myself. Never mind. It was just a thought. You can keep the yarmulke."

Charles thought she looked cheerful. He decided to forget the incident. She left quickly. As he passed the living room table, he laid a fifty-mark bill on the coffee table; he thought the extra ten marks would make her happy. He wanted to make her happy.

Esther Cleans Up

The next morning her footsteps beat in a furious percussion down the hall. She appeared in his doorway, babbled something about filthy and lazy, and how she could take no more. She disappeared.

"Look what happens to the bathroom when I don't lock it up!" she called. He trotted after her, impressed by her astonishing array of cosmetics. She was scrubbing the sink. "I've never seen such a mess!" Then the floor. She whirled around with her sponge until she knocked a shelf and all the beautiful women on the bottles and boxes toppled and spun off. He wanted to help her and picked up a container. But she snatched this out of his hand before he could even look at it and cried, "Get out of here!"

He returned to his room, sat down on his bed and reread a *Herald Tribune.* When she flounced in after him he pretended not to notice her.

"The worst dirt comes from coins," she said, putting a wet ten pfennig piece on the table. "Have you noticed how black your hands get from a wet coin?"

Inside Esther, a Mysterious Landscape

On a weekday the promenade along the lake was not overrun by families, and then Allerhand, who professed to hate the sight of children, took his assistant for a walk there.

"Isn't it glorious? One should be grateful for such a beautiful day," Johannes Allerhand said, his voice directed toward nature as much as toward his companion. She was thirty years younger than he, but he had insisted on straining with a blanket and the picnic basket, and she did not offer to help, for fear of annoying him.

"The trees, the sky, the water—Germany!" The water had a film of petrol. This did not discourage swimmers from dropping their clothes along the soggy banks of the lake and diving in nude, as if they had been overpowered by the same sentiments that wrenched at Allerhand. The two turned away from the water onto a dirt path that led into the woods. Soon they left the path, and with Johannes Allerhand leading, pushed through the underbrush until they reached a small clearance where the sun shone through. Allerhand spread the blanket. "Go ahead, lie down."

He took off his hat and shirt, and stood with his broad back and bald head facing her, chin up, eyes closed. "And I thought I was too old to feel this." He walked from tree to tree, touching the bark at his knee level.

When he found the scar in the wood he returned to Esther, opened the picnic basket, and took out a child's shovel. He dug a hole at the base of the tree beneath the mark. He did not exert himself, nor did he dig as casually as a child either; he frowned until his plastic shovel tapped metal, and then he scooped an ordinary container from the dirt.

Esther was no longer watching him; she had fallen asleep. He dusted off the box, opened it, removing a packet of West German passports which he leafed through with pleasure. He refilled the hole, fooling around with the earth for a while before he returned to the hamper and took out a bottle of wine. He sat down on the blanket at Esther's feet and drank greedily. Esther was watching him through half-closed eyes. She smiled.

"Nature gives me an appetite," he said. He leaned over and put his hand on her calf, running it down to take off her shoes.

Mother Exists

Charles's eyes were ravenous with appetite. He saw the light perspiration on her forehead and her upper lip. He watched for each effect that speaking and swallowing and breathing had on her scarred mouth and on her pretty teeth.

"What do you think about going back to America?" she asked. "Just spare me this mess and your staring at me all the time."

"Yes, I could go back to Oregon," he answered as he examined the way her hair fell over her shoulders. "Get my old job back right away."

"And what about the store?"

"Just keep it."

"That's not enough! You have to sign it over to me. But we can do that, all we need is a piece of paper, and you write down, 'Charles Allen sells his inheritance to Esther Becker for one mark.' We both sign, finished."

"I don't want to sign anything."

"What do you want? Read the sports page, of course. Eat, sleep, and regular bowels. Fit for the slaughterhouse," she said. "The Nazis would have tied you to a spit and roasted you! Look, let me write up a statement, all you have to do is sign it. You come with me this morning. That's what you wanted all along. Stare at me till you're sated. Stare and then sign."

She bought a *Herald Tribune* and opened it for him at the baseball news. He read in the car next to her. He could step out of the car without putting the paper down, estimate the location of the curb without losing his place on the page, and hold a door open for Esther, his eyes riveted to the text. "My mother lives here," said Esther. Then he looked up. They were inside an institution.

Esther's mother existed: small, straight, and wearing a fancy dress with lots of lace and ribbons. "Dressed like a Christmas present again, aren't you?" Esther said, approaching her from behind. "Vain till the bitter end."

Her mother heard but did not register the assault. Her name, Frau Becker, was printed on a button stuck into her lapel. She turned the pages of a magazine and did not stop when Esther came up to her. Herr Brumm, Fräulein Gierlich, and Frau Harzbach, sharing a table with her, also turned pages, although they were in the midst of heated discussion about food prices.

"Why do you still worry about prices," teased Esther, "when you no longer have to buy anything?" The pages of *Tip, Stern, Brigitte* flapped.

"It was cheaper in the past," said Fräulein Gierlich, "but it wasn't as easy to get. Potatoes you could buy, but meat? Hundred grams a week per person. A child can eat that for dinner. War! No meat during wartime. Terrible days, I'm glad they're over."

"Terrible days, with that Hitler fooling us. And afterward, even worse," said Frau Harzbach.

"But before the war, we had our own vegetable stand at Fehrberliner Platz," said Herr Brumm. "The higher-ups came to us after work. And lined up."

"But you have visitors, Frau Becker, crank your head around

and look!'' Frau Becker eased her head around like a ship making a wide turn, and regarded the figure standing next to her. ''Oh, it's you,'' she said, ''how nice. My daughter,'' she told the others, ''has come to visit me.''

''We know your daughter: Fräulein Becker, isn't it?'' said Herr Brumm, greedy to look at someone younger than seventy.

''With a friend, it looks like.'' Frau Harzbach pointed at Charles Allen. ''Nice young man. Look, Frau Becker, now turn your head to the other side.''

Frau Becker turned and stared. Then she nodded, in Charles's direction. ''*Ach*, that's better,'' she wheezed.

Ach, *That's Better*

Ach, that's better. Later, Charles Allen wondered what she meant. He had not thought of asking Frau Becker. After just a minute with the elderly, Esther was seized with such impatience that she had to say good-bye again. She bade her mother for a word alone at another table in the lobby.

From a distance, Charles saw how Esther took a pen and several pieces of paper out of her purse, and how she laid the pages down for her mother to sign at the bottom. Then Esther kissed her on the cheek, and left her abruptly. Charles watched Esther walk toward him, while in the background her mother took some trouble getting back up on her feet, looking uncertainly after her daughter. Charles waved good-bye. He could make out Frau Becker's look of surprise, and how she switched her cane from the right hand to the left, in order to wave back.

''Waving to an old woman is no great contribution to the

family business. If you want to get involved with me, then help us," Esther chided him. "Even my mother helps us. She signs everything. They never bother senior citizens. Too venerable. The entire generation. One doesn't want to pry into their thoughts."

Esther Organizes the Afternoon

In Die Schöne Heimat Esther and Baruch cornered Charles with a bottle of wine. No one mentioned the previous night's argument. They were intent on manipulating their quarry. They filled his glass. "Charles, you can help us with Father Renard's icon," said Esther.

"We've been wondering who can take care of that for us," said Baruch. "*Prost,* you're perfect, Charles. Father Renard isn't very curious, and the figurine is beautiful, it comes from a little church near Versailles. The twins took a four-day guided tour to Paris and spotted it there. Father Renard only likes to buy from the deceased, so we told him it comes from an estate. Pass the bottle."

"He can take it over to Saint Josef's right now. As Dr. Allerhand," said Esther. "Keep drinking, Baruch, so you keep your wits about you . . ."

"I'm no doctor," said Charles. "I'm not going to pretend at all. I don't know how."

Baruch's voice turned soft, wounded. "We've had no one to replace your father, someone who knows how to behave in a church. I got beaten up in school too, Esther, for making fun of Catholics." He made a sign of the cross and chanted, "I can play dominoes . . . Better than you can play dominoes . . . I bet you ten to one I can beat you at domino-o-o-es."

"Pretend, no. But I can shake Father Renard's hand, and genuflect, if that's what you mean." Charles gave in.

It was a simple game: Baruch was going to play chauffeur with Esther's Mercedes, and Esther was going to label the box "Estate of Stella Wanderling," and Charles was going to wash his hands and practice telling the mirror, "Charles Allen with the icon you ordered. My father couldn't bring it around himself, as he is unfortunately deceased."

He was not going to talk about the icon because he was not going to lie. As he scrubbed his bony, impractical hands, Charles looked in the mirror and reflected that the Yankees had traded their best second baseman and would live to regret it. Minutes later a car honked in front of the door. The Mercedes had arrived, with Baruch in a chauffeur's uniform. His neck bulged at the collar. He ran around to open the back door for Charles.

Father Renard's church was an emergency measure in red brick taken over by Rome during the "Hunger Years," the late 1940s when food for the soul was also in short supply. Its spire had once been a symbol of growth for the neighborhood and could be seen for kilometers. Now it did not affect the skyline of more than one block.

But a Mercedes made an impression. Turkish children gathered and kept their eyes on the Mercedes star. Baruch parked on the sidewalk, and the crowd grew. He stepped out and addressed the children, "Touch this once and I'll shoot your mothers."

The children backed off.

The church was empty, blue light filtered in through the modern stained-glass windows and candles flickered at the stations of the cross that circled the nave. The American made a sign of the cross. Baruch tapped his temples.

The church office might have belonged to any small administration. An elderly woman counted and sorted coins. "I make a mistake, I lose my head," she said.

Father Renard was looking through the receipts. He was a picture-book cleric: mild-eyed, fine-featured, with so little vanity that one could not define his appearance. "So you're Dr. Allerhand. Johannes Allerhand's son." He weighted the words so that they sounded like consolation.

"Die Schöne Heimat has supplied us for ten years now, and we're very satisfied. High quality, at reasonable prices. A bit short on the paperwork, it's like shopping discount. But again and again, a remarkable piece, an icon, a tefillin—we're ecumenical in our interests—a rood, what have you. We have the most beautiful chapel in Berlin. And now this Madonna. Let's have a look."

He waited at a kind of attention, the way he heard his confessions, stiff-limbed to keep from erupting into joy. Charles unpacked the icon. The Madonna was stocky, black hair rimmed her veil, her skin a bluish-white. She looked, Charles thought, almost like his own Jewess. "Beautiful," murmured the priest, and produced his wallet. "This one is for me privately."

Brotherhood

During a card game around Baruch's Galé table, Esther announced she had made a decision. "It's the Christmas season again soon," she said, "and I want to get out of the candle business." She dealt the canasta deck.

Charles Allen sorted his cards. His hand was exciting. "Start, Esther," he begged.

"I am always having good ideas for Christmas," Henry Rosen said, "sales schemes for houses. Last year it was: Give your loved one what she's always wanted, an extra room! And today I suddenly had an idea for celebrating the anniversary of the most Christian of occasions, a pogrom.

"The Jewish community has a new director. He'd love to make a spectacular show of pride for his members, boost morale, something visible. Why not candles? A candlelit march to commemorate Kristallnacht. Very chic."

The others had not yet put their hands in order. Charles was impatient. "I have a good hand. Will anyone play?"

"Oh Henry," said Esther, "if the Jewish community needs candles, I'd love to supply them. I'll expand our order, they can have a special price. After all these years when they were on such bad terms with Johannes."

"Esther, will you play?" urged Charles.

"Will I what?" snapped Esther. "You're a little idiot. Your father lost everything he had on Kristallnacht—and you're about to lose your good hand. Because we have to go now." She tossed her hand on the table. Charles Allen shuffled the cards together and scuttled to keep up with the others.

It was warm for late October, an evening for a drive through the city with the windows rolled down and the radio turned up. But it was a night to turn off the radio, turn off the headlights, and turn silently into the loading bay of a warehouse. More cars arrived with their lights dimmed.

They waited. Charles wondered at Baruch's stern, intent demeanor. When a jalopy arrived with six giggling Turkish women in Bavarian scarves, Baruch climbed out of the Mercedes and jerked his finger across his throat. Then their silence had something forced about it, as though they were faking quiet, one could almost hear them continuing to chortle in their heads.

The silence ended with a truck rumbling into view. Baruch stumbled around the yard backward, helping the driver steer into place. Finally everyone, including Charles, left their seats. He stood in the middle of a chain formed by the men to unload bundles from the truck, passing them from hand to hand, piling them at Esther's feet. She and Inge ripped open their thick plastic coverings and scooped out soft, dark fur coats. They held them briefly to their noses and cheeks, before handing them on to the six Turkish women who sat in a circle on folding stools and with dexterous hands removed the labels.

Charles's Long Night

Having committed his first crime, Charles Allen wanted to drink orange juice and then sleep. Esther granted him his wish. "If you want to, you can fall in love with me. I'm lonely, you know."

"I do not fall in love, any more than I fall into a sewer."

"And if I dyed my hair blonde?"

When he picked up the newspaper, she left the guest room. He put down the newspaper and stared at the door. Turning his head, he could see the high white door with the brass handle reflected as a white light in his window, and he could see it as a triptych in his dressing-table mirror. Faint as a tone from the back of the orchestra, he heard Esther reach her room.

She would be unzipping her dress now, he thought, her arm

crooked over her shoulder, her left arm pulling the dress straight at the back, thrusting out her stomach—he had seen his mother do it—and then the dress would slide off her shoulders past her knees and she would step out of it, in a white slip. Next she would be throwing back the covers of her bed. Charles read his newspaper.

He imagined her sleeping now. Charles had seen Woman Asleep. In public places, on park benches, at bus depots and at the swimming pool, they closed their eyes, they had no shame. He had seen his mother asleep in her bed, it had shocked him.

The Orioles had bought a mediocre first baseman; but so what!

Charles dropped the paper on the floor. He passed along the hall through Esther's plastic greenhouse, and drew up to the door of her bedroom. He pushed it open and stared. The street light outside penetrated the long white curtains and shone on her head. She was sleeping on her side, her black hair in a nest on the pillow, her hand in a fist next to her cheek. She looked very young. Then he retreated. He had seen something else. On her bedside table stood a glass of water, and in it, glowing, rested a set of white teeth.

So It Happened that Charles Began Spending His Afternoons with Esther's Demented Mother

From then on, winter laid siege to the city. The dead linden and oak leaves were raked into rotting banks, the damp air had a searing, chemical smell, the days flickered with a weak light that was trimmed back by the early afternoon.

The press noted the robbery of a truckload of fur coats, the driver had been drugged by two Turks who had serviced him at his regular gas station. He had never seen them there before, and would presumably never see them again. The event commanded no more than one newspaper paragraph. Esther clipped the article and laid it on Charles's dressing-table. She treated him as a roomer and friend. Her suggestive manner—the way she patted him on the shoulder, or touched his hand while making a point —no longer worried him after Esther confessed that her last roomer had been his father. Obviously having a man sleeping in her apartment meant nothing special to her.

At the end of October, Charles wrote the Mother Superior of the Order of the Immaculate Conception in Athens, Oregon, a letter asking forgiveness for his delayed return. His decision whether to keep the inheritance had to be made by the ninth of November, Kristallnacht. The coincidence outraged Esther, and she chafed about the officials from the Bureau of Inheritance who were historically callous enough to make this date a deadline for a Jew to make a decision about property. Charles began to look for companionship in someone who did not trouble him so much. He was becoming bored with Esther's constant talk about Jews.

So it happened that Charles began spending his afternoons at the old-age home with Esther's demented mother. He never thought of bringing her flowers or chocolates, he just showed up and read his newspaper while she leafed through her magazine. Occasionally they talked about Esther, who was busy preparing a final sale of Holy Land candles for the Christmas season. She was offering the candles so cheaply that parishes all over Berlin were putting in double and triple orders. Esther never signed any agreements, she passed on any documents that needed a signature to her mother who cooperated, confiding in Charles, "I'm too old to quarrel with her anymore; we've always had different opinions about everything." On occasion, Charles too would scrawl his name on a page, without ever asking her why; it seemed a small price to pay for his inability to decide what to do with the store. And the scope of this sale impressed him. Only the Jewish community had hesitated about buying the Holy Land candles.

It didn't interest Charles when, at the bar mitzvah of another community boy, Herr Rosen had broached the subject of "special" candles for the Kristallnacht commemoration to the new community rabbi. A band from Tel Aviv had just come on stage, the rabbi kept turning his head trying to clear the rock-and-roll out of his ears. He understood Rosen's undertone despite the decibels: the new rabbi could make a citywide impression with a big event using candles supplied from the Holy Land instead of an old Nazi factory in Fulda, candles borne in the hands of thousands in a march through downtown Berlin ending in front of the Jewish community center.

Although the image appealed to Rabbi Schwarz, canniness made him hesitate. Herr Rosen was so frustrated at his inability to make a deal that he promised to throw in a seventeenth-century menorah from Alsatia at a special price. Now the community chief couldn't resist. The community needed an impressive menorah. He had grown up in New York and he said, "Make me a reasonable offer on that menorah and you have a deal on the candles."

But Esther didn't want to sell the menorah. "It's from my birthplace, I'm not selling it."

"It doesn't belong to you, does it?" argued Baruch. "It belongs to Hans's son."

"Only after he accepts the inheritance. Until then, the manager decides what to do with the merchandise."

Rosen had come around directly to the store from the bar mitzvah. He called Esther crude names but the adjective that set everyone's head nodding in agreement was "ungrateful." Henry appealed to Baruch's superior judgment. "Talk her out of it, you're her friend." But Baruch didn't like to question Esther on business policy, and he said Charles should decide what to do with the menorah.

Charles wanted to shrug, say, "Let Esther choose," and reach for his newspaper. But her tenacity made him suspicious. The menorah was Johannes Allerhand's last acquisition for Die Schöne Heimat. Was she sentimental about his father? The thought disgusted Charles. "Schwarz can have it," he said. "What's the use of having it lie around here? For one thousand marks."

"Father Renard is the only reliable buyer," Esther battled. "And that menorah happens to be hot from a museum. Interpol is looking for it."

"There's one place they won't dream of looking," said Baruch. "And we have to keep on good terms with the community."

"But one thousand isn't enough!" cried Esther. "We can get twenty-five hundred or three thousand for it. It was sold at auction for ninety-five thousand. Money is all I have these days," she said bitterly.

"A thousand is enough," decided Charles.

So Rosen passed the menorah on to the rabbi with a fake bill of sale from Christie's and the stipulation that no attention must be drawn to it, questions were to be answered "no comment" until the old woman who had given it up, and who would be dreadfully offended, no longer lived. Rabbi Schwarz calculated that he needed one candle for each member of the community, and an equal number of visitors, optimism became the nth power in his calculation, and he ordered ten thousand candles, which amounted to half a ton.

In all, Esther ordered two tons of Holy Land candles which were shipped from Dresden with a special clearance from a corrupt official in East Berlin, crossing the border in a truck with Fulda license plates. Charles himself directed the truck to the different delivery points in Berlin, sitting in the caboose next to the driver accepting huge cash payments for the candles. When they had finished their rounds, he handed the East German a bank check from Die Schöne Heimat. The check, Esther told him later as she opened a bottle of champagne, was not covered. Charles, the accountant, should have known that. The check would bounce sky-high. There was nothing the candle company could do about it since accepting a Western check was illegal in East Germany. "You're up to your neck," Esther laughed, "in money."

It was the eighth of November. If Charles Allen did not reject his inheritance by the next day—anniversary of our humiliation," Esther called it—then he would own Die Schöne Heimat.

Charles left Esther and Baruch dividing bundles of marks into three piles. They insisted he take his share because they weren't scoundrels. He left his portion in plain sight on the same antique table where he had once attempted to make sense of his father's business, and excused himself, polite as an altar boy. Charles needed to know something.

At the old-age home, Frau Becker closed the magazine, hesitated, and then answered him. "The one she had before was much too old for her. I never knew his first name. He used to bring me chocolates. I think he was trying to charm me. In East Germany he brought me coffee. I couldn't say no to coffee, we had none. But I told him to keep his chocolate for himself. He was rather fat. He died. Esther told me that.

"I am not really on speaking terms with my daughter, but that's her decision. She has never been a good child. But times were hard, you know, when she was small. My husband felt so helpless and he never got over it. It was such a humiliation, what happened to us. Afterward he was not a man any more. I had to do everything. It's something I never talk about here. And my husband died of it, died of the broken heart."

"I know, Frau Becker," Charles said, recalling Esther's words, "how terrible it was for you being Jewish in Germany back then, Esther has told me how you had to hide in a haystack in Alsatia. Pregnant and alone. And all that. Terrified that the Nazis would find you when the baby screamed. I am—" He stopped. She had jerked forward in her seat, the magazine flopping off her lap, and was staring at him. "I am Jewish too," said Charles Allen, and he tried, covertly, by pretending to scratch his forehead, and then dropping his hand to his chest, to make a sign of the cross.

"Go, please," begged the old woman. "Esther tells everyone that story? Please, leave me alone now." She was trembling, her mouth hanging open. Charles fled.

Last Shopping Day Before Kristallnacht

Charles Allen left the old-age home just as the street lights were turned on, and shop windows began to sparkle. Soon they reflected the pulsating red of police lights. He followed this to the

Jewish community house where the Kristallnacht procession was just arriving. It proved a magnificent crowd of emotional people but not many Jews among them, they had stayed home in fright. Instead, students and their teachers, university societies, various SPD unions, and the entire Christian Democratic leadership came, each individual holding a thick, white, brightly burning candle. Traffic was chaotic, and the helpless drivers cursed the marchers.

The procession halted when it reached the front of the community house, dissolving into a crowd plied by policemen and a contingent of nicely dressed, earnest young men distributing leaflets about the Auschwitz lie. The crowd grew silent when Rabbi Schwarz appeared on the top of the stairs of the Jewish community house. Everyone knew he had lost his parents and all his siblings in Auschwitz. He raised the huge seven-armed menorah high over his head with its candles blazing. Silhouetted in black on the rooftop behind him lay the police sharpshooters.

Esther's Birth into a Mysterious Landscape

The reporters were already at the wall, alerted by the old man whose life's work was informing reporters of an escape. The reporters tipped the tipster handsomely; it was his only source of income, for the courts had refused to pay this embarrassingly prominent former official a pension. His name had not always been Schmidt, but now he had become well known as Wallwatcher Schmidt, and even if the times changed back again, as he often fantasized, he would have probably stayed with the new name.

The reporters slipped him small bills and considered him a

nuisance. He always hung around at the site of the escape, tripped over their equipment, and horned in on the honor. This time was no different. Schmidt and three photographers and a crowd of locals watched as the heavyset, elderly man in a gray fedora, who refused to face the cameras and refused to name himself, began digging frantically with a shovel at a particular point at the wall. The man who the press referred to as "the stranger" kept his back to the cameras so all they had to shoot was a hat, a short neck, and a huge, dark overcoat.

Meanwhile Schmidt was making such a pest of himself trying to help dig this tunnel that the photographers could no longer concentrate and lost precious seconds when they should have positioned themselves differently. They missed the moment altogether, which they knew was the high point of this particular escape, when "the stranger" reached his arm deep into the tunnel and pulled, steadying himself with one foot against the wall. In this position he strained as if he were pulling all of East Berlin through the tunnel.

Luckily the photographers were able to shake Schmidt off in time to get a shot when he succeeded in lifting out a raven-haired girl with a Star of David around her neck. She came out into freedom looking only into her rescuer's eyes, with an expression of trepidation and surprise the public could not fathom and attributed to the news photographers.

Esther and Charles Celebrate Kristallnacht

Poor Charles, chilled and frightened by the Kristallnacht festivities, hurried home. From the street he saw the yellow light of her warm living-room and Esther on a ladder hanging paper garlands in the window. Inside, the smell of roast lamb made him so meek that he allowed Esther to throw her arms around his neck and say, "Darling, we have to celebrate! Don't you understand?—We've bought ourselves a bit of financial security. Don't worry, the East Germans will never dare to prosecute. You and I are having guests. Like a normal couple. You have to pretend."

She tied a flowered apron around his waist, handed him a dish towel and instructed him so cheerfully in the fine art of drying dishes that he could not help wondering whether he had found happiness at last.

At seven-thirty the doorbell rang. Esther swore: it was too early, nothing was finished yet. But it was not one of the invited guests; it was Esther's mother, in thick shoes and an ugly raincoat, panting hideously. She carried a plastic shopping bag with a picture of a white baby seal on it and the inscription, "Save the Seals." Esther put her hand to her forehead. "*Oy vey,* what an honor."

Helga Becker entered, rummaging in the bag as she went. She extracted a piece of stiff official paper, a document. She stood in the middle of the living-room, holding this between her yellow thumb and forefinger. She squinted at the paper and read aloud, " 'Birth certificate of Margeret Becker, born 1944 in the Saint Gertrauden Krankenhaus in Berlin. No abnormalities. Father's profession: Lawyer. Member of the Party, and of the SS. Mother: Hausfrau.' Read it for yourself." She handed it to Charles Allen, canny and intent, continuing, "After the war he wasn't allowed to work so I supported us as a cleaning lady. I've had a hard life, I haven't always been in a good mood. And then at fifteen Margeret gets ideas. Insists her name is Esther. Dyes her beautiful hair black. Blond hair, she had, like an angel. It must take liters to keep it that color." She dropped a photograph on the coffee table under the bower. It showed a slender little girl with blond braids, sitting in the lap of a pale, tired-looking man.

Esther regarded her mother with detachment. Then she addressed Charles. "This is not my real mother at all. I didn't want to tell you because you are such a bunny rabbit: the Nazis found my real mother when I was born, and they murdered her.

"This is my stepmother, who has always hated me. She used to beat me. She knocked out my teeth when I was ten."

The two women turned to each other as if Charles himself were choreographing them: their profiles were identical.

For the first time since his arrival in Berlin Charles Allen showed emotion. He couldn't control his voice because a rage had punched up into his throat, and he cried, "Get out, and leave Esther alone!" He pointed his pale, weak, trembling hand at the door, he did not think how silly he looked in his posy apron. The old woman lost her nerve then. When she left, he slammed the door majestically behind her. He returned purposefully, and picked up the photograph of the child.

She was pretty, but where she smiled there were no teeth showing. There was a raw, red scar on her upper lip.

He put the photo down carelessly and moved toward the woman who had been his host for the past months, and as he went he pulled off his apron. His rage had reached his groin now. She tried to push him away. She put her small hands on his chest and pushed. Although he was tall, he was slight, but he was not to be stopped, the energy in him was burning a fuel of thirty-five years: he pulled her apart, her clothes, her clenched arms and legs, his actions ran their course on the plastic lawn like a simple motor: he raped her.

Charles Is Recognized

When Father Renard unlocked the church on the morning of the ninth of November and went inside to say good morning to his thuribles, pyx, relics and crucifixes, he saw the devil.

The priest refrained from using the name of the Lord in vain, stepped outside the church again where he leaned against the door, breathing heavily. The additional oxygen made him skeptical that the devil should trouble to come in his church. But he found no other explanation for what looked like a red tail. Unless he had hidden there after the Kristallnacht service the night before, with the intention of thieving, only to be locked in, a common thief perhaps, there must be another explanation for the red tail. Now Father Renard decided it was safe to turn on the coronas and look. The tail proved to be an old, red-wool scarf, one end dangling, the other stuck beneath the seat of a man sleeping propped up against a suitcase in a pew. At the ringing of Father Renard's footsteps, and the sudden light, the man opened his eyes. Father Renard peered at him. "Oh!" he cried. "It's you! Mr. Allerhand! Naughty boy, sleeping here. Just like your father used to do. In the morning I would hear his confession. It was always very interesting. But why the suitcase?"

To Father Renard's disappointment, Charles Allen's only words were of thanks, and then the "devil" left, red scarf wrapped around his neck, ends tucked into a thin raincoat. The weather had turned wintry. The priest watched him and saw how he stopped after a few yards to put on a peculiar white cap. After another few yards, he suddenly pulled the cap off again and flagged a taxi with it. As he was wrestling his suitcase into the car, the cap dropped into the street—Father Renard shouted, "Wait!" The taxi pulled away. The priest chased the car for a block, clutching the wet white cap, but to no avail. He would put it in his office for safekeeping.

When Father Renard dusted the sleeper's pew, he found a postcard there. It was stamped properly and addressed to the Office of Inheritance. Father Renard did not like to pry, yet he could not help reading the short text. But it was uninteresting, full of negatives, something about not accepting an inheritance and not wishing to know any more about it. The priest thought the young man's carelessness with his possessions should be punished, but mailed the postcard for him nevertheless.